"It's high time you were in bed."

Jonas glanced down at Robyn. "I'll see you in the morning. Good night."

"Good night." It was almost as though she had been dismissed. She made her way to her room and was soon lying in the darkness. *Barbara.* Of course it was Barbara. He was out there remembering the times they'd stood on the balcony together—the times he'd kissed her in the moonlight. Tears of anger trickled down to soak into Robyn's pillow.

You stupid idiot, she chided herself fiercely. *Your course is clear. Get his office in order, make sure his aunt is okay and then get yourself back to Sydney!*

WELCOME
TO THE WONDERFUL WORLD
OF *Harlequin Romances*

Interesting, informative and entertaining,
each Harlequin Romance portrays an appealing
and original love story. With a varied array
of settings, we may lure you on an African safari,
to a quaint Welsh village, or an exotic Riviera
location—anywhere and everywhere that adventurous
men and women fall in love.

As publishers of Harlequin Romances, we're
extremely proud of our books. Since 1949,
Harlequin Enterprises has built its publishing
reputation on the solid base of quality and
originality. Our stories are the most popular
paperback romances sold in North America; every
month, six new titles are released and sold at
nearly every book-selling store in Canada and the
United States.

For a list of all titles currently available,
send your name and address to:

HARLEQUIN READER SERVICE,
(In the U.S.) P.O. Box 52040, Phoenix, AZ 85072-2040
(In Canada) P.O. Box 2800, Postal Station A
5170 Yonge Street, Willowdale, Ont. M2N 6J3

We sincerely hope you enjoy reading
this Harlequin Romance.

Yours truly,

THE PUBLISHERS
Harlequin Romances

Boss of Brightlands

Miriam MacGregor

Harlequin Books

TORONTO • NEW YORK • LONDON
AMSTERDAM • PARIS • SYDNEY • HAMBURG
STOCKHOLM • ATHENS • TOKYO • MILAN

Original hardcover edition published in 1985
by Mills & Boon Limited

ISBN 0-373-02710-9

Harlequin Romance first edition August 1985

CHAPTER ONE

ROBYN Burnett shut the front door of the flat and went towards the house next door. As she went through her neighbour's gate she paused to gaze at the old building, and as usual she found something appealing about its timbered walls, its delicate tracery of cast-iron embellishments between the tall pillars and railings of the encircling veranda. Coolabah, as it was known, had been built at the turn of the century, its style giving it an air of dignified Australian solidarity which contrasted with the more modern houses in James Street, and particularly with the neighbouring brick flats where Robyn lived with Sally Dawson.

Coolabah was obviously too large for one person, yet it was lived in only by Mary Anita Hollingford, who had been a widow for less than a year. It had been built by her late husband's father, who had named it after a box eucalyptus tree which, he had declared, gave shelter from the hot Queensland sun and from the cold winter winds which swept the escarpment of the Great Dividing Range upon which the city of Toowoomba had been established.

As Robyn ran up the wide front steps the sun shot lights through her shoulder-length dark brown hair. It was September, yet the wind still held a bitter chill—a chill that was as cold as a broken heart, she thought whimsically, her mind turning unbidden towards Gregory Blake. The next moment she was pushing his image away, thanking heaven she seldom thought of him these days, but still aware that the experience had left her deeply scarred. No doubt Gregory had been left untouched. No doubt he was still trampling hearts as he danced along on his merry philandering way. The

5

emotional calamity had caused her to lose faith in all men. They were not to be trusted, and at least Gregory had taught her that bitter lesson.

She paused on the veranda to take in several deep breaths of the clear air that was almost heady with its high-altitude freshness, then she tapped on the front door which had been left ajar. Pushing it open a little further, she called, 'Are you there, Holly——? It's only me—Robyn!'

A voice called from the front bedroom on the left of the hall. 'Come in, dear—I was just about to have my afternoon nap.'

'I thought I'd look in to see that you're okay.'

'You're a dear girl. I was hoping you'd come—that's why I left the door open, although I know it's unwise. One never knows who might walk in.'

Robyn smiled at the slim woman lying on the bed, noting the fragile delicacy of the small hands. 'There's something you want me to do for you?'

Blue eyes gazed up at her. 'It's that desk again. I took one look at the horrible clutter and shut the lid! Bills to be paid, estate papers to be sorted, letters to be answered. The ones from New Zealand worry me most. Flora insists on getting regular mail from me. I know it's kind of my sister-in-law to worry about me, but no sooner do I write to her than bang—back comes more mail from her and I'm owing her a letter all over again. I suppose you think I'm being ungrateful to my brother's wife.'

'Not at all,' Robyn laughed.

'And as for all those get-well cards—they're only things that people toss into the mail, and I'm so poor at letter-writing. Yes—yes, I know it's the *thought* that counts——'

'Don't worry, I'll help you with them,' consoled Robyn. 'You still feel seedy after that horrible virus you had during the winter, but it's gone now and you're on the mend.' She hesitated, then asked, 'Would you like me to sort it all out for you?'

A grateful sigh came from the bed. 'Yes, please, you've done it so often for me and you're very quick at it now. I'm sorry to be such a ninny, but George used to attend to all the accounts. It was *his* desk and it really hurts me to sit at it. The memories come crowding all over me—they bear me down.'

'I understand,' Robyn said gently. 'Now you go to sleep.'

But Holly hadn't finished. 'And my opal earrings— would you keep your eyes open for them?'

Robyn's brown eyes reflected dismay. 'Those lovely opal earrings? Surely you haven't lost them?'

'I hope not. They must be somewhere.' Holly's expression became vague. 'I haven't worn them for months and I don't know what made me start thinking about them. They might be in a box in the bottom drawer of the desk—a sort of jewel casket.'

'You haven't searched in it?'

'No. It's a place where I keep a few odds and ends of old jewellery I seldom wear. When I bent down to open the drawer my head ached and I felt dizzy. I'd be glad if you'd find the box and look in it for me.'

'Don't worry—those earrings will be found.'

Holly closed her eyes wearily. 'Dear Robyn, you're so kind to me. You're just like the daughter I never had. What makes you so good to me? I've often wondered about it.'

Robyn searched in her mind for an answer. It would be tactless to admit that Holly reminded her of a pathetic bird with a broken wing—one lying on the ground waiting to be picked up—a helpless creature in need of assistance. Nor was it possible for her to admit that the aid she herself offered was an automatic gesture of compassion, something she did because it was her nature to do so. She became aware that Holly's eyes were upon her, the question still lurking within their depths, therefore, grasping at an answer, she said, 'Maybe it's because you remind me of my mother. She's about your age and build, but with more flesh on her bones.'

The blue eyes sent Robyn a shrewd look. 'I don't remind you of your mother at all. She's neither as inadequate nor as useless as I am—she can't be, to own three boutiques in Sydney.'

Robyn pulled the continental quilt about the thin shoulders. 'Now just stop worrying about why this, or why that. Concentrate on going to sleep and I'll go to the desk. When you wake I'll make you a cup of tea. And don't forget that Toowoomba's Carnival of Flowers begins in a few days. You'll want to be fit and well to come out and see the floral floats in the big parade.'

'Oh yes—they're always so beautiful—George always took me to see them.' The blue eyes closed.

Robyn closed the door quietly, then crossed the hall to the room which was still referred to as George's office. The walls were lined with books, and apart from the large mahogany rolltop desk there were comfortable chairs, a cocktail cabinet holding bottles and glasses, and a table set beside the window.

George Hollingford had been a grain grower and merchant, his acres of wheat, barley and oats being situated south of Toowoomba on the fertile Darling Downs. As Holly had admitted, it was not the first time Robyn had sat at his desk to sort out the piled conglomeration of papers which had been left there for later consideration; and now it seemed as if, from some vague place of limbo, George's spirit was again sending her to assist his widow, who had a strong dislike of what she called paperwork.

The main trouble lay in the fact that many of the envelopes held requests that were well over Holly's head, and she was unable to decide between what should be sent to the solicitor handling George's estate, the ones that should go to the accountant, and those she herself should pay. The estate papers were constant reminders that her beloved George, after suffering a massive coronary, was no longer with her. They upset her to such an extent that she threw them into the desk and slammed the lid on them.

For a short time Robyn opened the envelopes which concerned the estate. They were placed in a neat pile, and then she began sorting accounts from letters and get-well cards that had been left in a sate of chaos. They'd be lucky to be answered, she thought. And then she remembered the opal earrings.

Pushing the papers aside, she opened the bottom drawer and lifted a box on to the desk. As Holly had said, it was built in the form of a small banded casket, the mere sight of it stirring the imagination towards the contents of a treasure chest. She raised the curved lid to find it filled with a fascinating array of bead necklaces, earrings and costume jewellery fashionable in earlier years. There were crystal beads that glittered with a thousand colours, tinted pearls of pink and silver-grey, and she had just discovered the opal earrings when her heart leapt with fear as heavy footsteps sounded in the hall.

The front door had been left open, she recalled—and then she became aware of a man staring at her from the office doorway. Tall and of athletic build, she judged him to be about thirty. A lock of black hair fell over his forehead and beneath his dark brows his hazel eyes narrowed as he took in the sight of her sitting at the desk. 'Mrs Hollingford still lives in this house?' he demanded coolly.

The unexpectedness of his intrusion had almost taken her breath away, but she gathered her wits and remained calm. 'Yes, she still lives here. May I ask what right you have to come striding into her home in this manner?'

His strong square jaw seemed to tighten. 'It's more to the point that I ask what right *you* have to go through her desk. Where is she, by the way?'

'She—she's asleep. I don't wish to disturb her.'

'I'll bet you don't—if it's given you the chance to go poking into her private affairs.' He gave a short laugh that was completely lacking in humour. 'It's useless to deny it, because I can see that's what you're doing.'

'Yes—that's exactly what I'm doing,' Robyn informed him calmly.

His eyes glinted as they travelled over her dark brown hair with its slight wave, her soft brown eyes that had widened at the sight of him, and her sweet mouth that was now slightly compressed. They ran over the clinging cream trousers and top that revealed almost every curve of her slim but rounded figure. Well, who are you?' he demanded at last. 'Are you her secretary? I wasn't aware she needed the services of such a person.'

'No, I am not her secretary.' Robyn's reply came briefly. Why should she explain anything to this man?

'Well, who are you?' He snapped the question abruptly for the second time.

'What's it to you?' she countered evasively.

'Nothing at all,' he admitted. 'I've come to see Mrs Hollingford, not some stray female who rummages through her belongings.'

Robyn decided to ignore the remark. 'I told you she's asleep. She hasn't been well and she needs her rest. Perhaps you could come back later.'

He frowned. 'You mean she's been really ill?'

'She had a virus during the winter and it's taken several weeks for her to shake it off.'

'Then this is where you come in? You're a nurse?'

'No, I'm not a nurse. I live in a flat next door,' Robyn replied unthinkingly, forgetting her decision to tell him nothing.

'Ah—so you know her habits and felt it was a good time for a quick peep into the desk.'

She flushed angrily. 'How dare you make such an accusation!'

He strode towards the desk and examined the

colourful mass spilling out of the jewel casket. 'I suppose these baubles are your main interest. I'm afraid they're not very valuable. I doubt you'd get much for them.'

The insinuation infuriated her, but she managed to ignore it, although several deep breaths became necessary to keep her temper under control. Nevertheless her tone became scathing. 'If you really want to know, I was looking for a pair of opal earrings. I'm sure they're quite valuable.'

'Opals? No doubt they are. And I see you've found them.' His mouth remained grim.

'Yes, I found them.' She snatched them from the desk, gripping them tightly in her fist, her eyes mocking as she stared at him.

'I think you'd better hand them to me.'

'You—whoever you are—can go to the devil!'

He looked at her with sharp-eyed interest. 'My oath, you're a cool one! No wonder you're reluctant to tell me your name!'

'I see no reason to tell you my name.' Robyn piled the jewellery including the earrings back into the box and replaced it in the bottom drawer. 'Now, if you'll excuse me, I'll get on with the main task I have on hand—and if you're determined to see Mrs Hollingford you'll have to sit and wait for her to wake up, because I have no intention of disturbing her.' Then, deliberately ignoring him and wishing he'd go away, she continued with the sorting of the papers on the desk.

But the man did not go away, nor did he appear to have any intention of leaving the house. He went to the cocktail cabinet, examined its contents and poured himself a drink.

Robyn glared at him over her shoulder. 'You've got a nerve!'

He grinned at her. 'I've had a long journey—Holly wouldn't deny me a drink. Can I offer you something?'

'Certainly not. I don't drink other people's brandy

uninvited.' *Holly*. So he was on familiar terms with her, but at least this fact enabled Robyn to feel less apprehensive about his intrusion.

As she worked she refused to allow herself to become disconcerted by his presence, although it was difficult to remain calm. She knew he carried his drink to an armchair where he settled himself comfortably, crossing one long leg over the other, and from where she knew he watched her thoughtfully through narrowed lids.

Her fingers trembled slightly as she placed letters to be answered, cards to be acknowledged and accounts to be paid into various pigeonholes of the desk, and while her mind did its best to tell herself he wasn't there she remained acutely aware of his presence. At the same time she boiled with resentment when she thought of his accusations and his automatic assumption that she was a thief who'd crept in while Holly was taking her afternoon nap.

It was some time before he spoke again. 'May I ask what you're searching for?'

'Searching for?' The glance she slanted at him was disarmingly innocent. 'Money, of course. Isn't that what all thieves search for?' She turned again to the desk.

'I'm beginning to wonder if you are indeed someone who has the right to go through Holly's desk. Perhaps my initial suspicions were a trifle hasty.'

'Is that a fact?' irritation prompted her to snap. 'I must say it's a change to meet a man who's so rapid to see the light.'

His mouth became sardonic. 'Sarcasm doesn't become that pretty face.'

Robyn flushed slightly at the unexpected compliment, then returned to the work in hand. Concentration was becoming a struggle. He had a hard line of mouth, she thought, but there were also lines of humour about it. She noticed that the gold flecks in his hazel eyes flashed when he was annoyed, and that the white lines about his eyes indicated that he was an outdoor type who was in the habit of squinting against the sun.

There was also something about his voice that puzzled her. Deep and pleasant to listen to, it had a cultured quality with the barest trace of an accent that differed from the average Australian male tones, which were sometimes inclined to be harsh, high-pitched or even nasal. Was he an Australian? Despite her curiosity, nothing would allow her to ask the question.

The man's voice cut into her thoughts. 'Tell me more about Holly. Does she live alone in this large house?'

'Yes. The flats next door are close and I come in frequently to see that she's all right. On the other side of Coolabah there's a small cottage where a Mr and Mrs Bridge live. Mrs Bridge comes in each morning to do any cleaning that's necessary, and Mr Bridge, who's retired, mows the lawns and does the garden.'

'But she's alone at night? Wouldn't she be wiser to have a couple living with her?'

Robyn nodded. 'Yes, that'd be a wiser plan—but she says she's not yet ready to see other people sitting in George's fireside chair, or occupying his place at the table.'

'I see. Well, why don't you move in with her?'

'It's been suggested,' Robyn admitted coolly, 'but that would mean deserting my flatmate who relies on me to share the rent.'

'Or would it cramp your style when you're entertaining your men friends?' he asked.

She flushed angrily. 'I'll treat that question with the contempt it deserves. I do *not* entertain men in the flat. I'm not even remotely interested in men.'

'Are you trying to say you're allergic to them?' His tone held derision.

'Completely,' she snapped.

He gave a short laugh. 'I don't believe you.'

'Believe what you like—I couldn't care less.'

'Or is it possible the men find you boring? A prim cold icicle who'd rather die than be kissed,' he taunted.

She bristled with anger, then shrugged. 'I don't need any of them. My mind's fully occupied with my course at the D.D.I.'

'D.D.I.? What the hell's that?'

'D.D.I.A.E., to be more exact. The Darling Downs Institute of Advanced Education. I'm doing an art course there.'

'Art course? You mean you're learning to paint?'

'Yes. Unfortunately the course finishes in another couple of months. I've been working at it for three years.' Why did she bother to tell him these facts? she wondered.

'What'll you do at the end of it?'

A worried frown creased the smooth forehead. The same question had been nagging at her for some time. 'I—I haven't made up my mind. Perhaps I'll be able to find a job in Toowoomba.'

'Toowoomba isn't your home?'

'No. My parents live in Sydney, at least my mother lives there.'

'And so does the man who has caused your allergy towards the entire male sex.' The hazel eyes had become shrewd.

'Yes——' Her eyes flashed with anger. 'Will you kindly mind your own business! It's something I don't talk about.'

'Okay—okay, you're sure touchy about it. I suppose you'll finish the course with qualifications of some sort and then find yourself a job as an art teacher.'

'I don't want to do that. I'd prefer to keep art as a hobby and go back to my former office work. I've had clerical training—I worked with a firm of account-ants——' She stopped, again wondering why she offered this information. Next she'd be telling him that her father had helped finance her three years at the Institute and unless she could find a job that would enable her to pay her share of the rent she'd have no option but to return to Sydney. This wouldn't have been so difficult if Gregory's home hadn't been in the same suburb as her own, and if the most convenient morning bus to the city wasn't one of a group which he also caught.

She became aware that the man had refilled his glass and was examining the contents of the bookshelves. He then returned to the desk, picked up the pile of papers referring to the estate and carried them nearer the window.

'I see she's still got old Wills running the place,' he remarked, glancing at a signature.

'You've got a colossal nerve!' Robyn flared at him. 'Those papers contain Holly's private affairs——' She leapt from her chair and made an effort to snatch the bundle from him.

'I can see they refer to bushels per acre in various areas of the Coolabah property.'

'Give them to me at once—how dare you poke your nose into them—they're to go to the solicitor——'

'Or more likely to the accountant for tax assessment?'

'It doesn't matter where they're to go—they're not for your curious eyes.' She stretched out her arm in a vain attempt to reach the papers which were held aloft, the action taking her so near to him her small rounded breasts brushed his jacket.

'A little closer and you might get them,' he grinned.

'Give them to me——!' she panted.

'See if you can get them,' he taunted. His free arm went round her waist, the papers were dropped to the desk, and then both arms were holding her against his body. He stared down into her face. 'Tell me your name.' It was a command rather than a request.

She shook her head. 'Get your hands off me or I'll—I'll yell blue murder!'

'And wake Holly? I thought you wanted her to sleep.' A firm hand in the small of her back pressed her even closer to him. His eyes ran over her face as though taking note of every feature. 'Tell me your name,' he commanded again.

She glared at him in defiance. *'No!'*

'Very well.' One hand came up to hold the back of her head in a firm grip while his lips descended upon her own in a kiss that sent tremors racing through her body. It seemed endless, and for some reason she was powerless to struggle against it, but at last he raised his head. 'Your name——?' he murmured.

She remained silent until, realising his lips were about to find her own again, she capitulated. 'It's—it's Robyn Burnett,' she almost whimpered. The hold on her loosened and as she wrenched herself free her hand came up swiftly to deal him a stinging blow on the cheek. 'How—how dare you!' she gasped, her face scarlet with fury.

'Don't tell me you didn't enjoy that little reminder of what it's like to be kissed by a man,' he jeered.

'*Enjoyed*——? You—you great hulk of male ego——' Fuming, she became lost for words.

'You're overdoing things,' he retorted, watching her narrowly. 'It was only a kiss. You sound like a real man-hater instead of someone who's supposed to be merely allergic.'

'Yes, you can say I'm a real man-hater,' she hissed bitterly. 'I distrust the lot of you!'

'One would imagine you'd had much experience with the opposite sex,' he drawled.

'I needed only one experience, thank you. It left me anything but amused. I doubt I'll ever put my faith in another man.'

'Well, you won't get the chance to put *me* to the test. I'll not be around these parts for long.'

'Thank God for that. When do you leave?'

'When I've accomplished what I've come to do.' Then, reverting to the former subject, 'All the same, I don't believe you spend your time sitting in a flat and that you never go out with a man.'

'What you believe means nothing to me.' Robyn's legs were shaking as she sat down at the desk. A sudden weakness came over her, causing her to rest her head on her hand.

'One kiss has knocked you flat?' he asked derisively. 'You're making far too much out of a small incident. Here, take a sip of this—it might make you feel more normal—more like a *woman*,' he added with a sting to his words as he poured a small amount of brandy into a crystal glass.

Her hand shook slightly as she took it from him, a horrible suspicion that perhaps his accusation was correct growing steadily within her mind. Was she being a fool? Had she allowed the episode with Gregory to sear her soul and warp her judgment for all time? His voice cut through her fears.

'This flatmate of yours—is she also a man-hater?' his lip curled. 'If so you must be a pathetic pair. I mean, with you it seems to go so deeply.'

'Sally's doing a theatre course at the Institute,' she told him briefly. The thought of Sally as a man-hater caused a brief smile to touch her soft mouth. 'Sally and I are not really close friends,' she admitted. 'We have different values and opinions, but we fit in well when it comes to sharing a flat.'

For some unknown reason she resented his interest in Sally, and as she returned his gaze she became aware of the brooding question in the hazel eyes. Then, coming as a blessed relief, the silence between them was broken by Holly's voice calling from the bedroom.

'Are you there, Robyn? I'm awake, dear——'

Robyn left the desk and crossed the hall, followed by the tall stranger. 'Kindly wait in the hall,' she snapped, trying to bar his way into the bedroom.

'Don't be silly,' he laughed, pushing her aside, his manner changing abruptly as he marched into the room. 'Surprise, surprise!' he called gaily.

Holly sat up in bed, staring at him wide-eyed. '*Jonas*—my dear, dear Jonas—is it really you? What are you doing here?' Words seemed to fail her as she sat clasping her hands.

'I've come to check up on you, of course.' He sat on the side of the bed and hugged her.

'You knew I'd been ill? Well, not really *ill*—just laid low.'

'One or two things made me suspicious. Your letters had become few and far between, and when they arrived the writing was shaky and the sentences a trifle rambling. They were so unlike you I decided to pop across the Tasman to see what was what.'

Holly began to laugh. '*Dear* Jonas, how very like you!' Then as Robyn placed an extra pillow at her back and a pink knitted cape about her thin shoulders she said, 'You realise who this man is, Robyn?'

'No, I haven't the foggiest notion. So far he hasn't had the grace to introduce himself.' She kept her voice cool, refusing to look at the man whose eyes now seemed to hold mocking amusement.

'He's my nephew, Jonas Ellingham from New Zealand,' Holly cooed fatuously, making it obvious she adored the wretched fellow.

'Really?' Robyn refused to be impressed. 'Would you like me to make some tea?'

'Oh yes, please, dear. I'm so glad we've got some of those nice cookies you made for me.'

Robyn went to the kitchen, her thoughts in a whirl. So this was Jonas Ellingham, of whom she'd heard Holly speak so often. This was the man who now owned the estate that had been Holly's home before she married George Hollingford and moved to Queensland. What was its name? *Brightlands*. The word leapt before her eyes.

Holly had spoken of it many times, and now snatches of her reminiscences came back to Robyn. Fertile riverside orchard land near Hastings in Hawke's Bay, she'd said. When the rising sun peeped over the rolling hills beyond the river its slanting rays sparkled on the water, dazzling the eyes to such an extent it was almost impossible to look in that direction.

Dewdrops about to fall from leaves glistened like hanging diamonds, Holly had said. Delicate cobwebs festooning the hedge shone against the dark foliage in lacy white relief. Everything was so colourful, especially when the fruit trees were in bloom. First came the clouds of snowy plum blossoms, followed by the bursting pink of nectarines and peaches, and next came the flowering of the pears and apples to complete the blossomtime cycle of the orchard.

Everything was so *bright* that Holly's mother had declared there was no other name for the place. And here, in person, was the master of these bright lands. Why hadn't he admitted to being Holly's nephew when he'd first walked into the office? Why had he allowed her to imagine he was an intruder? No doubt the sight of her at his aunt's desk had given him a nasty jolt, but he could have discovered the situation without jumping to the conclusion that she was dishonest.

She tried to recall Holly's words concerning her brother's son. 'Handsome, my dear, that's what he is,' she'd declared one day when raving on about his virtues. But she hadn't admitted to his domineering attitude—his puffed-up arrogance, his overbearing self-esteem and male chauvinism. Oh yes, it was all there.

Robyn became aware that the man had followed her to the kitchen and was standing close behind her. Her hand shook slightly as she poured the boiling water into the teapot.

He examined the tray. 'Only two cups? Aren't you having tea with us?'

'No. I'm sure you and Holly will have private matters to discuss.'

'We have—but they can wait. You'll have tea with us.' Again it was an order rather than a request.

Mutely she placed a third cup and saucer on the tray while he opened a jar and extracted several more cookies. 'She's very thin,' he remarked. 'Doesn't she eat?'

'I'm afraid her appetite's rather small.'

He peered into the refrigerator. 'Not much food in the place. I'd better rectify that state of affairs. I don't intend to starve while I'm here.'

'I usually do Holly's shopping for her,' Robyn explained. 'She writes a list of what she needs, but you must understand that a person living alone doesn't keep much food in the house because it's easy to buy fresh vegetables when the supermarket's so near.'

'You'll have to show me where it is. By the way, my aunt's been telling me you've been most helpful to her. I'm grateful to you, of course, but I can't help wondering what's behind all this philanthropic assistance.' His eyes became penetrating.

She sent him an angry glare. 'You've definitely made up your mind there *is* something behind it?'

He shrugged. 'There's a reason for everything, and no doubt you'll have your motive for helping her,' he commented dryly.

'Then you'll just have to fathom it out for yourself,' she snapped. Irritated, she turned and lifted the tray from the bench.

He moved to take it from her, and as he did so his hands covered her own. She felt the firmness of his grip and for a moment she stared at him in startled anger before snatching her hands away.

He noticed her action. 'I can see that you sure hate my hide.'

Her brows rose as she allowed her eyes to run over his masculine length from head to foot. 'You're mistaken. Your—*hide*, as you so aptly put it, isn't even on my list for consideration.'

'No?' Gold lights glittered in the hazel eyes. 'Then we'll have to see about that, won't we?' His eyes narrowed and the lights disappeared. 'Besides, I owe you something for that slap on the face. Nobody does that to me and gets away with it.'

'Oh? You'll give me a swift one under the ear, I suppose?'

'Not exactly. I'm not in the habit of striking women.'

'Not physically perhaps, but verbally you're certainly an expert at delivering hurtful blows.' She was being a fool, she told herself as she led the way along the hall. She was allowing him to rile her and to get under her skin. Her best plan was to ignore him and with luck he'd soon be leaving and on his way back to New Zealand—and Brightlands. It was a nice name, she decided reluctantly. It was a name that conjured up visions of sunshine and flowers.

When they returned to the bedroom Robyn noticed that Holly's eyes shone, her cheeks had taken on a healthier hue, and it seemed as though this odious man's arrival was acting like a tonic to give her a new lease of life. She smiled at Robyn. 'I've been telling Jonas all about you, dear. He admits he learnt your name while I was sleeping, so I don't suppose there's need for further introductions.'

'None at all,' Robyn responded crisply, yet with a feeling of dismay. Had Holly told her nephew *all* about her? Had the unhappy affair of Gregory been mentioned? She hoped not, and rather regretted having told Holly about it. Her eyes held a question as she glanced at Holly, who was gazing with rapture at Jonas, and again she wondered if she was being hypersensitive over the episode with Gregory. Pushing the thought of him aside, she became her usual practical self. 'I've made out cheques for those larger accounts. If you sign them I'll pay them when I go to buy stores for the flat.'

'Thank you, dear.' Holly paused before sending an uncertain glance towards Jonas. 'Did you say stores? Have I enough food in the house for a hungry man?'

'Definitely not, Aunt,' Jonas cut in with a short laugh

before Robyn could answer. 'Apart from a small piece of cold chicken and the remains of a casserole your fridge runs a good second to Mother Hubbard's cupboard. I believe hers was completely bare.'

Holly looked about her in a vague manner. 'My purse, Robyn—perhaps you could get me a few things——'

'Forget your purse, Aunt. I'll go with Robyn to see what the supermarket has to offer.' The hazel eyes bored into the soft brown ones as though daring her to refuse the offer of his company.

Robyn found herself unable to protest against his plan. It would upset Holly, and this was something she had no wish to do. She was genuinely fond of her frail elderly neighbour and never questioned the reason for her own instinctive wish to protect her from emotional stress of any kind. 'Why not come with us, Holly?' she found herself suggesting. 'You've had your rest, and the outing would do you good.'

'No, thank you, dear. I'd prefer to stay home and attend to the guest room. By the way, did you find my opal earrings?'

'Yes. They're in the box in the desk—just as you thought they'd be.'

'Thank heavens! I'm so glad I asked you to search for them. George gave those earrings to me——'

Robyn sent Jonas Ellingham a level stare of cold triumph, thankful that Holly had voluntarily cleared up that small point. He made no comment. Instead he returned her gaze with a cool glare that seemed to indicate that he was completely unimpressed by the explanation.

Holly, oblivious to these chilly optical exchanges, peered through the net curtains at the window. 'Is that your car out there, Jonas?'

'It's a rental. I arranged to have it waiting for me at Brisbane after the flight from Auckland. If Robyn will come with me she can guide me to the supermarket.'

Robyn indeed! she thought with a sense of indignation. How dared he assume he could use her name on such short acquaintance, especially on one that had been marred by his insinuations concerning her honesty?

'You'll go with Jonas, dear?' Holly watched her anxiously.

'Yes—of course.' Robyn forced a bright smile. Holly mustn't be allowed to suspect her feelings towards this beloved nephew who obviously meant so much to her. 'But first I must go to the flat.'

She hastened next door and changed from the casual cream suit to a burnt orange knife-pleated skirt and matching jacket that sent a warm glow to her cheeks. She ran a comb through her hair, applied fresh make-up and stepped into her dark brown high-heeled shoes. Surveying herself in the long wardrobe mirror, she remarked aloud, 'You *fool*—you're dressing up for him. What's got into you? You know you hate him.' Then slinging a bag over her shoulder she slammed the front door of the flat and forced herself to walk without haste to where he waited beside the rental car.

CHAPTER TWO

THEY drove along James Street where the avenue of dappled-bark plane trees stood like solemn sentinels. Robyn directed him to turn into the long straight stretch of Ruthven Street which led to the main shopping area, the tense silence between them being broken only when they reached the town were flags flapped and multi-coloured streamers across the road swayed in the breeze.

As they stopped at traffic lights Jonas indicated the decorated awnings and flower-filled shop windows. 'Why all the gaiety?' he asked. 'The whole place seems to be dressed up.'

'It's Carnival of Flowers week, an annual event for which Toowoomba is famous,' she explained. 'There are competitions between the small, medium and large trade windows and decorated awnings, not to mention between the private gardens.' She was glad the silence that had hovered like a dark cloud had been broken, as she had never been one who remained in a state of sulkiness.

She looked at his hands as they rested on the steering wheel. Tanned and capable, they were like the rest of him, well-shaped and with a hidden strength. She'd already felt the force of those hands—in the small of her back. The memory of it sent a flood of colour rushing to her face, and turning away before he could observe it she said crisply, 'We'll get rid of these estate papers and then I'll pay the accounts.'

Later, with the last receipt in her bag, she said, 'The supermarket I usually drive Holly to is out of town. We go back along Ruthven Street.'

His brows rose. 'You drive her? Doesn't she drive herself?'

'No. She's become nervous of the traffic.'

'But I saw a car in the garage—a small blue Wolseley.'

'That's my car. Sally uses the garage at the flat, so Holly allows me to park my car in her garage.'

'What happened to George's Daimler?' he asked.

'It was sold. It was through the Daimler that I met Holly. One day I saw it being driven away and a short time later I noticed her walking about the garden. I could see she was weeping, so I went out and asked if she was all right—although I could see she wasn't. She explained that her husband's car had just been sold and the sight of the empty garage was another reminder of his death——'

'I can guess what happened,' he interrupted on a harsh note. 'You suggested that her best plan was to have another car in the garage, and then you asked if you could keep your one there.'

She sent him a surprised glance. 'Yes, it did happen like that. Did Holly tell you?'

'No—but it's easy to see the picture. Quite a little opportunist, aren't you?' His eyes had narrowed and the smile that was meant to soften the words was grim.

Taken aback, Robyn retorted angrily, 'That's how it happened, except for one omission. I offered to pay rent for the garage.'

He gave a derisive laugh. 'No doubt. But you were probably sure that a wealthy woman like Holly wouldn't bother about rent for a garage.'

'Wealthy?' She was startled. 'I've never looked upon her as being particularly wealthy. She doesn't live in an opulent manner.'

'Then your clerical training's letting you down. You must be naïve not to realise that all those grain-growing acres out on the Darling Downs must mean something. Surely you know she's worth more than peanuts.'

'To be honest, I've never given the matter a thought.'

'No? That's difficult to believe.'

Deeply hurt, Robyn stared straight ahead as they drove through the Ruthven Street avenue of camphor laurels with their rounded tops and glossy yellow-green leaves, and the jacarandas that were almost ready to burst into clusters of blue-mauve blossoms.

Jonas's next words came as another surprise. 'Well, whatever your motives, my parents will be grateful for any help you've given my aunt.'

'Tell them to think nothing of it,' she responded coolly. 'She's a sweet person, even if she is a little helpless at times.'

'Helpless? Holly? You've got to be joking!'

She sent him a wide-eyed glance. 'You don't know your aunt very well, do you?'

'I know her well enough to fear her actions when an affectionate young miss gets her round her little finger.'

'And that's where I've got Holly? Now who's joking?'

'I'm afraid I'm being quite serious. However, I've no intention of voicing my suspicions to her as I think it'd make her most unhappy. I'll let it ride—for a while.'

'What, exactly, are your suspicions, Mr Ellingham? Suppose you come clean and tell me what's bugging you. Let's get everything out in the open.'

'Okay, you've asked for it,' he shrugged. 'I've a very strong feeling that you're nothing more than a cunning little gold-digger who plans to creep into an elderly woman's confidence for the sake of what she can get. There now, is that plain enough for you?'

She gave a bitter laugh. 'Plans? Aren't you a little late? I think I already have Holly's confidence.'

'That state of affairs can be rectified.'

'Also, aren't you being a trifle unfair? You've only just arrived and you don't know me at all. What's made you jump to these horrible conclusions?'

He was silent for a few moments. 'I think it was the sight of you at the desk,' he admitted at last. 'It gave me a shock to see someone going through my aunt's papers while she slept, and to see you examining that box of jewellery was enough to rouse all my suspicions, whereas if you'd just been writing a letter——'

'But I wasn't just writing a letter—and as you hinted earlier, I must have a *motive* for helping Holly.'

He frowned and remained silent until he said, 'Well, it stirred an instinct that shouted that all was not well.'

'It made you feel I have her in the hollow of my hand?' Robyn was assailed with the desire to giggle. Despite the fact that his remarks had been so insulting the situation was so very ridiculous it was impossible to take it seriously.

'Yes, I suppose I do suspect you've got her in the hollow of your hand,' he admitted, 'but don't worry— you'll be given the chance to exonerate yourself. You'll be given the opportunity to prove whether you have her interests at heart—or your own.'

'I will? That's interesting. How am I to do that?'

'You'll see when the time comes.'

As they turned into the parking area of the shopping complex enlightenment dawned upon her. 'I believe you hope to enlist my assistance,' she declared.

'I might.' His tone was noncommittal.

She swept him with a cold glare. 'You're very optimistic. What makes you imagine it'll be given to you—especially after the accusations you've made concerning my honesty?'

He pulled up in a vacant space, then turned amused eyes upon her. 'You feel so antagonistic towards me?'

'*Antagonistic!*' Her lip curled. 'What an understatement! I *loathe* you. The sooner I see the back of you the happier I'll be!' She flung herself out of the car, slammed the door and ran into the supermarket as quickly as her high heels would allow.

Tears stung her eyes, but by the time she had wrenched a shining chrome-plated wire trolley from the tightly wedged row she had regained her temper. She moved swiftly among other shoppers, pushing the trolley between the high shelves and freezers, and snatching at the groceries she needed. As she turned a corner she almost bumped into Jonas, who looked completely lost as he gazed about him like a man in a wilderness.

'Where the devil do they keep the bread?' he demanded testily.

She took pity on him. 'It's along at the end. Holly prefers the Roggenbroff fibre bread in the blue plastic bags.'

He followed her about the supermarket, pushing the trolley he had acquired. Dairy products, cooked fowls, pies and vegetables were tossed into it with complete disregard for cost until Robyn was moved to protest.

'Holly will have a fit when she sees this lot! That meat pie is far too large for her use.'

'Then you'll have to help us eat it,' he remarked nonchalantly.

She moved to change it for a small size, but he was too quick for her. His hands gripped her wrists and his gaze held her own. When he spoke his words were clipped. 'A continual battle seems to rage between us. Can't we call a truce—for Holly's sake? It won't be for long, I promise you.'

'Very well—for Holly's sake.' Robyn released her grip on the pie and sent him a dazzling smile. 'How long did you say you'd be staying round these parts, Mr Ellingham?'

'I didn't say—except that it'll be for as long as it takes me to do what I've come to do, but I told you that before. And let me warn you—every time you call me Mr Ellingham I'll kiss you.'

She stared at him coldly. 'You wouldn't dare!'

'Wouldn't I?' His eyes glinted and a smile hovered about the hard mouth. 'Tempt me and see what happens. Here in the supermarket would be a good place to try it on.'

'Don't be a fool,' she snapped, aware that her colour had risen.

'Now we know who wouldn't dare,' he teased.

Aware that her pulses were beating slightly faster, Robyn flounced aware from him, her pleated skirt swirling in a circle as she swung round.

'I suppose you know you've got lovely legs,' he commented dryly. 'They're shapely all the way up——'

She ignored the remark and made her way to the row of check-out desks, where her few purchases were put through quickly. But the trolley filled by Jonas took longer to be checked and paid for, and as she waited for him to push it towards the car she pondered his words. He would be here for as long as it took him to do what he had come to do, he'd indicated. What had he come to do? she wondered.

When they returned to the house Holly was up and dressed in a dark blue woollen dress that emphasised her grey hair but did nothing to disguise the frail state of her thin body. She looked at the pile of groceries Jonas dumped on the kitchen table, her blue eyes widening with dismay. 'Dear Jonas,' she quavered, 'you're always so generous. When do you expect me to use all this food? Just look at all these vegetables!'

'Food is obviously what you need, Aunt.'

Robyn left them to argue about the payment of all he'd bought, and as she went along the hall she heard Jonas explain that this was the first time he'd pushed a trolley round a supermarket and that the temptation to fill it had been overwhelming. She smiled and agreed with Holly. Yes, he *was* generous. Then, startled, she realised that this was the first kind thought she had sent in the odious man's direction.

As she went to the rental car to collect her own purchases she noticed that Sally's car was now in their garage. The sight of it brought her to a decision, and without further hesitation she went to the rear of Holly's house, moved her own small Wolseley from the garage and parked it on the concrete in front of the flat. She then slid behind the wheel of the rental car, turned the key which had been left in the ignition and drove it round the back to park it in Holly's garage.

'There you are, Mr Ellingham,' she said aloud. 'The garage is all yours.' She suspected she was being childish, but the action was worth the satisfaction it gave her.

As she carried the purchases into the flat Sally's voice called from the bedroom. 'Is that you, Rob? Where have you been?'

'To the supermarket for our stores. I went with Holly's nephew—he's here from New Zealand.'

'A *man*? Are you telling me you went to the supermarket with a *man*? I don't believe it.' The information was enough to bring Sally to the doorway, and Robyn felt the usual inferiority complex, the same old sense of insignificance when in the same room with her, because tall, beautiful blonde Sally was everything that Robyn longed to be.

And now Sally's blue eyes held an extra sparkle of interest. 'What's he like? Don't tell me—let me guess. He's exactly like Holly, a sparrow with skinny legs—an undersized little twerp.'

Robyn laughed. Sally's reaction to the handsome Jonas Ellingham would be interesting to watch, she thought. 'How would I know what his legs are like?' she asked at last.

'How, indeed?' the other girl agreed, then, with a touch of exasperation, 'Really, Robyn, you do waste a lot of time in that house next door. What do you expect it to *give* you?'

A tender light flashed into the brown eyes. 'I know exactly what it gives me. I like Holly and it gives me pleasure to help her. Is there something strange about that?'

'Huh! It's a heap of codswallop. You must know she's loaded and you'd be a fool not to be hoping to get *something* out of all your efforts.'

Robyn's eyes became troubled. 'In what way? What do you imagine I expect?' It hurt her to hear Sally echoing the words and thoughts of Jonas Ellingham. Was this how her association with Holly appeared to most people? Did everyone look upon her as a cunning little gold-digger?

'I think you expect your name to appear in her will,' Sally accused with sudden conviction. 'Any day now you'll be running the old dear to her solicitor's office—and personally I think you've got more brains than people give you credit for.'

Robyn turned to face her angrily, but before she could speak there was a knock on the front door, which had been left ajar. They both swung round to face Jonas Ellingham, whose grim expression betrayed the fact that he had overheard the latter part of their conversation. Robyn flushed a deep red, but Sally remained calm, her eyes narrowing with sudden interest as they took in the sight of the tall broad-shouldered figure clad in the well-cut suit.

When Robyn had introduced them he said, 'My aunt would like you girls to join us for evening meal. It seems I went quite mad in the supermarket. The pie I bought is far too large——'

'—Therefore would we help you eat it,' Sally cut in, her manner suddenly gay and vivacious. 'Yes, thank you—we two poor students will be most grateful.'

He laughed, catching her mood. 'Your flatmate says you're studying to be an actress.'

'Actress! How I love the sound of that word.' She went on to tell him about the course offered by the Institute while he responded with a few questions concerning it.

Robyn listened to the exchange a little enviously. It was so easy for Sally to be uninhibited, to chatter with a complete stranger as though she'd known him for years. As for the insufferable Jonas Ellingham, he appeared to be a different person. He was smiling and polite, and not at all like the irritable male she'd met in the house next door. But then he hadn't discovered Sally searching through his aunt's desk.

She said, 'I'm sure you two can find plenty to talk about. I'll go next door and see if I can help Holly with the meal.' She found Holly peeling potatoes and took the sharp-bladed plastic peeler from the thin claw-like hand. 'I'll do them,' she said. 'You set the table and find some flowers for a centrepiece.'

'Thank you, dear,' the older woman sighed, then, with more animation, 'Don't you think he's handsome? Have I told you he's my brother's only child? I'm longing to hear about Brightlands, and I can't help wondering about the girl—Barbara.'

'Barbara?' Robyn asked idly.

'I remember her only too well because she made me feel so old and insignificant. Flora's last letter said that she was spending a great deal of time at the orchard, and I'm curious to learn if there's anything between them.'

'You mean between Jonas and Barbara?'

'Yes. Jonas is a most eligible young man, you know.'

But Robyn was hardly listening as her mind was on the couple next door. Why were they taking so long to make an appearance?

Holly went on, 'My brother Robert and Barbara's father have been old friends for years, but I don't think Flora and the girl's mother are so very close.'

'How long is it since you've been there?'

'George and I flew across to New Zealand a short time before he died. I hate flying—I'm so nervous.'

Robyn was busy in the kitchen with meal preparations when Jonas and Sally arrived, and as she worked she listened to the voices floating through the door from the living room. Holly was making a valiant effort to talk to Jonas, but it was a losing battle as Sally continued to monopolise his attention by describing some of the many subjects offered by the Institute and taught within its ten major buildings.

Again the fact that her own course was almost finished thrust itself upon her. Mother had been right to persuade her to take it, but almost every day the question of what she would do when it ended rose to nag at her. She turned to switch the steaming vegetables to a lower heat and found Jonas standing beside her, a bottle of still red wine in his hand.

'A corkscrew, please,' he requested. 'I'm sure you know where everything's kept in this kitchen.'

She realised the latter comment had a subtle double meaning behind it, but she ignored it and found the required article.

'Sally's been telling me about you,' he went on, his deep voice deceptively casual. 'She says you're a very level-headed person.'

'I'd hate to be thought scatty,' she admitted, wondering where this trend of conversation was leading.

'Then Sally's correct when she says there's a purpose behind everything you do?'

'Isn't there a purpose behind the actions of most people? I've yet to see anybody do anything without a reason of some sort. To what, in particular, was Sally referring?'

'She told me your main purpose in leaving Sydney was to get away from your lover.'

'My—my *lover*——?' she gasped, her face scarlet. 'He was *not* my lover—at least, not in the way you mean. Sally had no right to suggest such a thing!' Rage made her hands shake.

'She also told me that your reason for taking your art course was to help you forget him.' His hazel eyes became penetrating as they held her gaze. They were like gimlets boring into something soft and pliable which at that moment was her mind because she was unable to think clearly.

'So—so what?' she muttered defiantly.

He was watching her narrowly. 'Has it been successful? Have you been able to forget him?'

'If it's of any interest to you, I've wiped *all* men out of my life.' Robyn sent an angry glance towards the living room.

He read her thoughts. 'Don't blame Sally, because it wasn't her fault. I asked her point-blank about it and she merely answered my questions.'

She bristled angrily. 'You've a confounded nerve to poke your nose into my affairs! What business is it of yours——?'

He was unperturbed. 'Is there a napkin I can wrap round this bottle?' he asked as though changing the subject. 'It's a fine Queensland wine from the Granite Belt and guaranteed to loosen all tongues. Perhaps it'll take the stiff-backed attitude out of some of us.' He sent her a sidelong glance.

'You're hoping to learn further secrets?'

'I'm not interested in your secrets. It's your help I need.'

'My help? I don't understand.'

'You will—when the time comes.'

'You made a similar reference earlier,' she reminded him. 'I presume it's getting close—the time, I mean.'

'Very close. During dinner, in fact.'

'I see. And the wine is supposed to soften me to the extent of agreeing with whatever you have in mind? Perhaps I should warn you that wine has been known to bring out an argumentative streak in me, Mr Ellingham. I'm told I can become quite stubborn.'

'I can believe it because that kissable mouth is belied by a rather obstinate chin. However, you were warned about calling me Mr Ellingham in the supermarket, remember?' His eyes glinted as he looked at her.

'You—you wouldn't dare—not in Holly's kitchen——'

'Wouldn't I? Just watch me.' He placed the bottle of wine on the bench and although she backed away from him his arms went about her in a firm grip.

'I'll—I'll scream——' she warned as he bent his head.

'It'll be lost in your throat,' he murmured, finding her lips with his own. Then, almost abruptly, the embrace ended as he said, 'Come into the living room. I've poured a sherry for you. In any case, you've spent enough time in the kitchen.' He moved to take her arm, but she snatched it away, sidestepping before his hand could touch her.

During the meal Jonas divided his attention between his aunt and Sally. Robyn he almost ignored, apart from passing her the salt or refilling her wine glass, and if anyone noticed his silence towards her they gave no sign of it. Sally's eyes hardly left his face, while Holly's mind was occupied by questions about Brightlands.

'I know you own the place,' she said. 'Robert wrote and told me he'd signed it over to you when he retired.'

'Yes. Father was forced to retire for health reasons. At first he continued to work about the fruit trees as usual, until Mother put her foot down. Retirement meant retirement, she declared, especially for a man under doctor's orders, so one day she went off and bought a house at Westshore.'

'That's a seaside place a few miles away,' Holly explained to Robyn and Sally. 'What does he do there?'

'He pushes a boat out and goes fishing, while Mother worries until he comes home.'

'And your mother—Flora—is she—is she just the same?'

'I presume you're asking if she's still as managing as ever. Yes, Aunt, she still rules the roost—hers and mine.'

'This means you're living in the Brightlands homestead alone? I can hardly imagine Flora allowing it.'

Jonas laughed. 'Don't worry—Mother soon had everything under control. Do you remember Barbara Dalton?'

Holly's mouth tightened. 'Oh yes, I remember Barbara. All that red hair and those green eyes——'

'That's right. She must have impressed you, for you to have remembered her so clearly.'

'Wasn't she one of the seasonal pickers?' asked Holly.

'Yes. She has an aunt who wasn't very happy living with her in-laws, so it was arranged for her to take over the running of the homestead. Her name's Mrs Kerr. She knows all the pickers and packers and their relatives, and the moment we need labour she's on the phone.' He took a sip of wine and leaned back in his chair. 'And Alf—do you remember Alf? He's still there acting as a major-domo,' Jonas said, as though deliberately steering the subject away from Barbara.

Holly gazed at him fondly. 'And so you're really the master of Brightlands. All you need now is a wife who'll grace the place—somebody kind and gentle, like—like——' She stopped abruptly as though suddenly aware of what she had been about to say.

'Yes, Aunt? Somebody like—Barbara, perhaps?'

But Holly was not to be trapped. She looked directly at Jonas and said with an edge to her voice, 'Someone who'll love you for yourself and not because you're the owner of Brightlands, which we all know is a most desirable property.'

'Actually it's now even more extensive than when you were last there. Since taking over from Dad I've bought extra land and I'm now growing large areas of asparagus and tomatoes. Peas, beans and sweet corn are also being grown for the two big canning factories which are in the district.'

Holly's eyes widened. 'You've been able to finance all this extra land?'

'Well, I've negotiated with the bank. A couple of good seasons should see me clear and I'll be away laughing. Dad offered to lend me the money, but I've no intention of interfering with any of his investments. This is something I'm doing alone.'

Robyn was unable to resist a question. 'Suppose the seasons are bad? Holly once told me that Hawke's

Bay's a place which can be troubled by severe droughts. What happens if your crops fail?'

The dark brows drew together as though the question angered him. 'It'll then be necessary for me to take another look at the financial situation,' he admitted coolly.

But the question still hovered in Robyn's mind, because she had caught a brief expression in his eyes which puzzled her. Had the others noticed it? she wondered. It was almost as though a flash of apprehension had lurked beneath the confident exterior he so boldly presented to the world.

Her experience gained when working with the firm of accountants had taught her that it was easy for people to become over-enthusiastic about a project, to go in too deeply and then have to start looking for extra finance. Was this the true reason for the visit to his aunt? Of course—*he wanted money.* No wonder he'd been so quick to suspect and resent her own association with Holly! Anger began to surge within her, but she compressed her lips and said nothing. Time would tell, she told herself.

'I hope you'll be careful, Jonas.' Holly's voice was tinged with anxiety. 'I'd hate to see you reach the state of having to raise a large mortgage on Brightlands.'

'He'd never do that,' Sally exclaimed. 'Jonas is too clever to get into financial difficulties.' She beamed at him.

He grinned. 'Thank you for your confidence, beautiful lady.' Then, as if in gratitude for the remark, he flattered her by saying, 'The deep violet of that dress emphasises the colour of your eyes.'

Sally glowed with pleasure. 'I'm told it suits me. Our theatre director said it makes my eyes look like Toowoomba violets. Did you know that the violet is the floral emblem of Toowoomba?'

'You're working on a play at present?' asked Jonas.

'Yes—it's called *Outward Bound.* It takes place on

board a ship where all the passengers are dead. Quite hilarious, really.'

Holly was shocked. '*Hilarious?* To be *dead*? Is it supposed to be a farce? There's nothing funny about death, especially after you've lost a dear one.' Her eyes became moist.

Jonas patted her hand. 'Now don't get upset, Aunt. It's only a play, and sooner or later we all have to die. The main point is to make the best of things while we're still alive on earth.'

'Like keeping good health and not getting gripped by a virus in the winter,' added Robyn, surprised to find herself agreeing with the man she had decided she detested.

'Exactly.' He refilled her glass and turned to his aunt. 'You've been very fortunate to have had Robyn's assistance over the last few months, but no doubt you're aware that her course finishes at the end of November.'

Holly nodded. 'Dear Robyn—she's been so good to me.'

'And no doubt you're also aware that it's possible she'll leave the flat that's been so conveniently placed for you both?'

Holly looked at Robyn, a faint frown creasing her brow. 'Do you think you'll go away from here?'

Robyn sent a curious glance in the direction of Jonas Ellingham. Something other than a request for money was on his mind, she felt sure. 'I don't know,' she answered warily. 'It's a bridge I'll cross when I come to it.'

'I suppose it'll depend on the sort of job you'll be able to find and just where it'll be,' Holly mused.

Sally uttered a laugh that was slightly derisive. 'Robyn doesn't need to worry about a job. She can go into one of her mother's boutiques. So much for art!'

'I don't want to do that,' Robyn said sharply. 'It'd mean going back to Sydney.'

'And you don't want to do that?' Jonas put in softly.

She sent him a direct stare. 'You're leading up to something, aren't you? You have the air of a tiger about to pounce.'

'You're right. I'm leading up to my aunt's situation. It's possible she's been fortunate in having you next door, but what happens to her if you go away? I can now see she's one who needs help, but we can't expect Sally to take over where you've left off.'

Sally became alarmed. 'Me? Do you mean I'd take over?'

'Certainly not. You're busy learning lines—training to be the leading flower of Toowoomba, although there's nothing shy and head-hanging about you. Anyone less like a violet I've yet to see.' Jonas tempered the words by sending her one of his rare smiles.

Holly became impatient. 'What are you going on about, Jonas? Will you please be sensible and tell me what you're trying to say. I know it's something to do with me.'

'Okay, Aunt, here it is. I think you should come home to live in New Zealand. There's a place for you at Brightlands.'

Holly stared at him as the suggestion registered with her. 'Home? You're forgetting, Jonas—*this* is my home!'

'Deep down you know that Brightlands will always be home.'

She shook her head. 'I'm afraid that's no longer true. Dear Jonas, don't you understand? This is my home. This is Coolabah, the home to which George brought me as a bride. I couldn't leave it.' She looked about the room as though seeing things for the first time. 'It would mean selling the house and everything in it. It'd be sacrilege. George would be furious!'

Jonas controlled his exasperation. 'My dear aunt, *George isn't here.*'

She sent him a direct stare. 'Oh yes, he is. His spirit is everywhere—in this living room, in the office——'

'For Pete's sake, Aunt, don't tell me you believe his ghost's trotting about the place.'

'I don't know that I actually believe in ghosts, because I've never seen one, but I *do* know that there are times when George feels very close to me.'

'Okay, if you say so.' He shrugged and allowed the matter to drop. Nevertheless his eyes held a gleam of concern.

Later, as Robyn stacked plates into the dishwashing machine, he leaned against the bench and spoke to her in a low voice. 'I presume you can now see the way in which you can help my aunt?'

She decided to be obtuse. 'I'm not sure that I *do* see.'

'You can persuade her to return to New Zealand.'

'I can? Why should I do that?'

'For her own good, of course. It also gives you the opportunity to prove which concerns you more—her situation, or the feathering of your own nest.'

'How dare you make such a suggestion!' she flared angrily. 'If you want my co-operation you'd be wise to watch your words. This isn't a decision to be jumped at in five minutes. I'll have to think about it.'

'I *thought* you'd take that attitude. I *knew* you'd be perverse.' He gripped her hands, holding them tightly. 'Now listen to me, Robyn. I need your help and you're going to give it to me. Do you understand? You'll do so because you'll see it's the right thing to do.'

'I might—and I might not,' she snapped, wrenching her hands away. But as she gazed up into his coldly determined face she knew her heart was thudding.

CHAPTER THREE

SLEEP eluded Robyn that night, and at one o'clock she was still twisting restlessly, lying first on one side and then on the other. At times a soft breeze stirred the lacy curtains, moving them so that she was able to see countless stars glimmering down from the blackness of a velvety sky, but as she gazed up at them the constant twinkle did nothing to soothe the confusion in her mind, or erase from it the face of Jonas Ellingham.

She was being a traitor to herself, she decided crossly. The fact that he'd held her hands and has asked for her help had caused her to revert to the state of a twittering teenager—she, who had vowed she was finished with all men for all time. Earlier in the day his kiss had infuriated her. The temerity of the man—a *stranger*! But now when she recalled the incident she went hot all over—her mouth went dry and her breathing quickened.

In an effort to control her wayward emotions she reminded herself that she had already been warned against handsome men. Hadn't the lesson with Gregory taught her that few of them were to be trusted? Didn't the majority of them imagine themselves to be God's gift to the female sex and that women were there to be used in one way or another?

Now that indignation had made her think a little more clearly she realised that it was Jonas Ellingham's plan to use her. Not in the same ego-building way that Gregory had used her, but in a more cunning and subtle manner which would result in herself guiding events along the path he wished them to take. In this instance it was to persuade his aunt to move to New Zealand where some of her capital could possibly become invested in one of his mad schemes at Brightlands.

Well, she'd have to know a lot more about the place and think about it for a long time before she was sure of it being the best course for Holly to take. In the meantime she'd keep Gregory's image before her mind. It would serve as a brake in the unlikely event of her finding herself weakening beneath the persuasive powers of Jonas Ellingham.

Gregory Blake—what heartbreak he'd caused her! She gazed beyond the curtain to the stars and recalled the day she had met him. She supposed it had really begun with the first sight of him, when she had noticed the tall auburn-haired man at the shelter where she caught the bus to the city; but little had she known she would meet him within the next few hours when the elderly accountant led her into the office of the new junior partner who had joined the firm that day. She recalled standing still and staring with amazement because there, behind the desk to greet her as his secretary, was the Greek god from the bus stop.

It had been pleasant working with him, and as the days passed Robyn had become aware of an inner secret excitement. She knew that he called her in from the outer office with surprising frequency and for any trivial reason that came to hand, and before long their friendship had developed to the stage where he took her for evening drives in the small car he left at home during the day.

For reasons he called sentimental he preferred to pick her up at the bus stop, his explanation being that this was the place where he had first set eyes upon her, and away they would go, across the Sydney harbour bridge and along the North Shore where he would park on a headland and gaze at the Tasman Sea.

Moonlight had shimmered on the waters as he had told her he loved her, and later they had run along the beach, their bare feet splashing the ripples that broke along the edge of the sand. Gregory had taken her dancing in strange remote places on the outskirts of the city, and for dinners in dim candlelit taverns that nestled in odd corners far away from what he called the maddening crowd.

She had been so happy, Robyn recalled, and had begun to visualise herself as the wife of a rising young consultant in a well-established firm. Yet he persisted in keeping their love a secret, and because of this there was no suggestion or mention of a ring. He wanted to be alone with her, to look at her, to hold her—and she knew she must be patient. It would be in one of his favourite bizarre places that he would ask her to marry him, she felt sure, but although she waited hopefully the words she longed to hear never emerged from his lips.

And then the crash came. It happened one evening when Robyn expressed the desire to go to a restaurant that had become popular because of its spectacular floorshow. It was right in the middle of the city and Gregory had been most reluctant to go near it. But by this time Robyn had become tired of what she was beginning to look upon as Gregory's sleazy little backyard dumps, and for once she was determined to eat in a more sophisticated environment. She had put on her most glamorous dress and had pleaded with him until at last, somewhat sulkily, he had agreed to take her there.

They were being led to a table when a woman left a party of friends and approached them. Robyn recalled that she had been a few years older than herself and had lines of bitterness etched about her mouth. 'Gregory darling,' she had cooed, 'I'm so glad your late work finished in time to bring your secretary to join us.' *She was his wife*.

Robyn never knew how she got through the rest of that nightmare evening, and even now the memory of it had the power to make her cringe until she felt physically ill. She had sat at the table as Gregory's secretary, who had been working late, but from the way the rest of the party treated her she realised that each and every one of them *knew* the situation only too well. The women were cold to her and the men were careful to ignore her, making it obvious that they looked upon her as Gregory's latest little bit of crumpet, which, of course, was exactly all she had been.

When she reached home she had burst into her mother's bedroom to weep and tell her the story. Rachel Burnett had listened with love and sympathy. She was an older edition of Robyn who kept herself alert, and being a practical businesswoman she viewed the situation with a calmer sense of proportion.

With her arms about Robyn's shaking form she had said, 'Darling, I know how you feel, but I also know how his wife feels. I learnt the bitterness of that situation when your father left me to live in Melbourne with that unmentionable woman. Thank heavens I had the boutiques to keep me sane. Now then—you're not going back to that job. How about going into the North Shore shop? They can do with extra help there——'

'The North Shore—oh no, that's the last place!' Robyn had wailed. The North Shore where the beach sparkled, where the sea pounded againt headlands and where Gregory had said he loved her. No, she couldn't go anywhere near the North Shore.

Rachel Burnett had looked at the tears streaming down Robyn's pale face. 'Fresh fields are what you need,' she had said with perception. 'Somewhere a long way from Sydney and with something entirely different to occupy your mind. Now then, what about taking an art course?'

Robyn had shot a surprised glance at her mother. 'Aren't you forgetting I'm already taking watercolour lessons with Mrs Gibson? It was your own idea.'

'Of course I haven't forgotten. Mrs Gibson's been most helpful to you, but I'm not happy about your progress with her. Your work isn't clean enough, and neither is hers, for that matter. It's the old story—people who are good at pencil sketching often fail when it comes to putting on colour. I doubt she'll ever get you to the stage of selling good paintings.'

Robyn had managed a smile. 'Dear Mother—always with an eye to business!'

'And why not? I'm a businesswoman. But we're talking about *you*. You can draw well—which made me think you should learn to paint—but I fear you won't get far with Mrs Gibson.'

Robyn's face had shown dismay. 'I thought you liked that last still life of oranges and grapefruit.'

'Let's face it, dear, I was being *kind*,' said her mother. 'You're still pleased with what you do because you haven't yet reached the state of being critical about your own work. Painting is a hobby you'll enjoy for the rest of your life. Learn to do it *well*. Get the *know-how* from the right place.'

And so the decision had been made, with application for enrolment being sent through the right channels. The special entry requirements to the course consisted of a practical drawing test which Robyn passed with ease, although her folio of previously completed work was looked at with reservations; however, the following February saw her settled in a flat at Toowoomba and ready to begin her art course at the Darling Downs Institute of Advanced Education.

In the meantime Rachel Burnett had written to Robyn's father. She had explained the situation and called for his financial aid, whereupon he had amazed both Robyn and her mother by coming to light with enough money to guarantee Robyn's rent for three years. But now the period was nearly finished and she couldn't expect her father to be paying out further large sums. She must learn to stand on her own two feet.

When she woke next morning she felt tired and heavy from lack of sleep. It was almost as though the reminiscences of past events had wearied her beyond endurance, but at least they had brought her to her senses by reminding her that few men were to be

trusted. Even her own father had been unfaithful to her
mother. The reminder had been timely, and she was
now sure that no matter how much electricity sparked
from Jonas Ellingham, his touch would leave her
unmoved.

She spent only a short time over breakfast, then she
snatched up a folio of work and made her way out of
the door before Sally could observe the tiredness about
her eyes. The small blue car started without any trouble
and within minutes she was sweeping round the corner
of James Street, then speeding between the Ruthven
Street camphor laurels and jacarandas. As she passed
the large supermarket Jonas Ellingham's face leapt
before her eyes, but she pushed it away as she turned
right and drove up the rise to the Institute.

It was good to be here, she thought. It was sure to be
one of those days when it was easier to work at the
Institute where there was so much going on around one,
instead of at home where one's thoughts would be in
danger of wandering towards a certain man in the
house next door.

She did not return home before late afternoon, and
even then she forced herself to continue with the project
that had occupied her during the day until a knock at
the door disturbed her. Startled, she guessed it would be
Jonas, and was annoyed to feel the blood rushing to her
face.

Casually dressed, he was immaculate in a pale buff
safari suit which looked as if it had just left the pressing
room of a laundry. The jacket had been left open
sufficiently to reveal a tanned muscular chest with its
light covering of short dark hairs, and, staring at them
in a semi-hypnotised manner, she knew they would be
as soft as silk beneath her touch.

'All alone?' he drawled, walking in uninvited and
examining the long room which was three-quarters
lounge before it switched to becoming a kitchen at the
far end. A bathroom and two bedrooms opened from it,

the larger being occupied by Robyn because she had a quantity of art clutter to contend with, yet despite the array of pastels, boxes of paints, canvases and blocks of watercolour paper stacked against the wall, it was as orderly as she could make it.

Jonas paused at the table and opened her folio.

'You've got a nerve!' she exclaimed angrily.

'Yes, haven't I?' he grinned, leafing through her work. The sketch of a house on a hill, its wide-fronted veranda held by numerous pillars, caught his interest. 'You copied this from an illustration?'

She was indignant. '*Copied* it? Of course not! It's Harlaxton House, one of the early Toowoomba homes. I sat in the car and sketched it, but I need to strengthen the hill foreground and check it to see that the perspective's correct.'

He propped it against the back of the settee, then stepped away to view it through half-closed lids. 'It looks okay to me. Your work is very pleasing—I like it.'

Robyn suppressed a smile. 'Thank you. You're saying nice things to me. I wonder why?'

He frowned, sending her a sharp glance. 'What do you mean?'

'Until those kind words you've been full of accusations and nasty suspicions, but now there appears to be a change. What can it mean? However, I'm sure you didn't come in to examine my work.'

'No, I came with a request. Holly is keen for me to watch the sunset from Picnic Point, wherever that is. She wants you to take me there—if it's not too much trouble.'

She stiffened. 'Holly knows the way. Why doesn't she take you?'

'She says she becomes confused with many of the streets. I'm beginning to suspect she's very good at becoming confused. It makes people leap about to do things for her.'

Robyn sprang to Holly's defence. 'I don't believe that for one moment. It's just that she lacks confidence in her own decisions and she likes to be told which is the best course to take. For years she did as George directed, and now that he's gone she's lost unless somebody points the way.'

'Then you'll promise to point her across the Tasman?'

She laughed. '*Now* I know why you said nice things about my work, but I'll promise nothing.' She turned away, disappointed that his praise of her sketching had been merely an angling for her assistance. Why did men imagine they had to flatter?

Jonas gripped her arms and spun her to face him. 'Can't you see it would be better for her to be near her own people?'

The feel of his hands sent a shock through her. She wrenched herself free. 'Please stop—you're hurting me. I'm not used to being manhandled!'

He released her abruptly, his tone changing as he said, 'Sit on the settee. It's all right, I have no intention of raping you. I just want to talk to you.'

He sat down in a relaxed manner, his arm along the back of the settee and one long leg crossed over the other. Robyn sat beside him, almost on the edge of the seat, and for some intangible reason found herself unable to look at him. Could he tell that her pulses were racing?

'For Pete's sake can't you sit on the seat? You'll be slithering off in a minute.' His arm went round her waist and jerked her beside him, the close contact with his body sending the blood rushing to her face. 'What's the matter?' he demanded as she drew back. 'Are you afraid of me?'

She gained control of herself. 'Of course not, but you'd like to think that, wouldn't you?'

He gave a short laugh. 'What makes you so sure?'

'Your domineering attitude tells me your ego needs constant feeding. You just have to be *boss*!'

He gave a sigh of resignation. 'Somebody has to lead the way in the right direction.'

'The right direction—for *whom*?'

His eyes glinted as they sent her a sharp glance. 'Are you hinting at something? Come on, out with it—what are you trying to say?' The glint in the hazel eyes had changed to a hard glare.

Robyn flushed and retreated, finding it impossible to admit that she suspected his reasons for wanting Holly to go to New Zealand. 'My thoughts are my own,' she said coolly at last.

And then her blood rushed even more swiftly as, unexpectedly, he took her hand. Turning it over, he stared down into the palm before his penetrating gaze raked across the petal-softness of her complexion. 'A lovely face, an astute mind—yet capable hands,' he remarked. 'They don't always go together. Such hands usually mean common sense. Are you endowed with common sense, Robyn?'

'I hope so.' She found herself staring at the crease on the side of his cheek and at the thickness of his black well-groomed hair. It would be nice to touch, she thought.

'Perhaps you can tell me—if my aunt became really ill how many friends apart from yourself would rally round to give her the assistance she'd need?'

'Very few, I suppose, but of course she'd go into hospital.'

'In that case common sense should tell you she'd be happier where relatives could visit her and attend to her needs. It should tell you what's best for Holly.'

'It also enables me to remember her solicitor's advice.'

'*Solicitor's* advice?' The dark brows shot up. 'What was that?' he demanded sharply.

'To sit tight for twelve months.' She became aware that his fingers were gently twisting the curled ends of her hair as it rested upon her shoulder, and that if she turned her head her cheek would brush his hand. She also knew she should move away from the closeness of his body, yet she felt powerless to do so, therefore she ignored his touch and concentrated upon Holly's situation.

At last she said, 'Holly told me that when George died she felt she couldn't live in the house without him. She planned to move into a flat, but her solicitor warned her not to make a change of any sort until twelve months after his death, otherwise she'd be liable to make a mistake and do something she'd regret.'

'The twelve months have almost passed,' he pointed out. 'Will you promise you'll try to guide her thinking along the right lines? The right lines for *her*, of course.'

'Only if I'm sure they *are* the right lines.'

'Fair enough. At least you'll promise to give it careful thought?' He glanced at his watch. 'Is it time to leave for Picnic Point, or will it mean too much interruption to your work?'

'I'll come now. This can wait until later.'

He stood up and was about to move towards the door when he happened to glance through the open doorway of her bedroom. A sketch on the wall caught his eye. 'That's Coolabah,' he declared in what was almost an accusing tone.

'Yes—I just happened to do it one day.'

His brows drew together as though the fact irritated him. 'I can see you're mighty keen on the old place.'

'Well, its white walls and pillars give it such atmosphere. Yes, I like Coolabah very much,' she admitted, seeing no reason for not being honest about it, yet sensing that in some subtle way his manner had changed towards her.

'I suppose I'm being a fool to expect any help from you. I suppose I can forget about it. Common sense— huh!' His voice had become harsh as he glared at her in sudden anger.

Robyn was bewildered by his abrupt change, but

refused to show it. However, the reason for it seemed clear enough and she forced herself to send him a singularly sweet smile. 'Are your previous impressions of me raising their ugly heads? Please don't bother to deny it or to disguise your suspicions, because I know that, despite your honeyed words of a short time ago, you still think I'm a gold-digger and out for all I can get. Why not be honest about it?' Her voice began to shake slightly.

'Time will tell,' he snarled, glaring at the sketch of Coolabah.

'That's right—and you'll just have to wait and see.'

Robyn was conscious of bitter disappointment. She was sorry the momentary truce between them had flared again to open hostility. The few minutes of compatability had been pleasant, even if they'd been so brief, but what else could she expect? Men were like that, she'd found. They were nice on the surface, but with strange and untrustworthy attitudes simmering below.

As she followed him through the door she paused to glance at the sketch which seemed to have caused his change of attitude. It was a pen and wash with only a small amount of colour in its clear blue sky, grey roof, green trees and foreground. But the sight of it had obviously upset Jonas, and again she realised that his suspicions of her motive for helping Holly went much deeper than she had thought.

Did he really believe she had hopes of being included in Holly's estate? Could he possibly imagine she was aiming to acquire Coolabah itself? The whole thing was quite ridiculous, although common sense forced her to realise it was a situation that would be used to advantage by many.

But Robyn herself knew she was not using the situation to her own advantage. Not once had she ever calculated the benefits or gains that could come to herself, and the knowledge that Jonas had placed her squarely in this category acted like a knife wound to her pride and self-assurance. By the time she'd taken her seat beside him in the rental car she was feeling utterly depressed and ill at ease.

She longed to cry out that he was wrong about her—he was being unfair—she didn't want him to look upon her as a brazen gold-digger; instead, she wanted him to *like* her just as she knew she liked him. Yes—to herself she had to admit she liked him.

Her mind in a whirl, she directed him along different streets until they reached Tourist Road and the pine avenue leading up the rise to Picnic Point. 'It's really a gigantic headland on an eastern spur of the Great Dividing Range,' she explained as they drove into the tree-sheltered area with its closely shaven lawns and bright gardens. For some unknown reason she was still feeling nervous, and subconsciously she knew that the proximity of Jonas was affecting her.

He parked the car near the kiosk, and as they walked across the grass she almost jumped as he unexpectedly took her arm. Her tension grew, flooding her with an inane desire to chatter, and pointing to a tall structure, she said. 'That's a water tower. It's known as the Mushroom because it's shaped like one. People look for it on their way home from Brisbane because it's the first thing they see as they approach the Range. And over here is the Puppy Memorial. Come and see Puppy——'

She led him to where the gunmetal figure of a Pomeranian dog had been mounted on a sandstone base. Still conscious of his grip on her arm, she went on, 'He was owned by the drum major of the Toowoomba Thistle Pipe Band. Every year the band led the parade of floral floats in the Carnival of Flowers, but it was Puppy who led the band. It's said he trotted along sedately, looking neither left nor right, and quite unperturbed by the noise of the crowds. If the procession stopped, Puppy stood still and waited for it to move on again.'

'Puppy? Didn't he have a name?' Jonas pulled her closer to him as they examined the statue, his fingers gently entwining her own.

His touch sent tingles through her body, but she managed to say calmly, 'No—he was just Puppy. You can see he wore a little tartan rug. Unfortunately he was killed in a traffic accident, but the people never forgot him and this memorial was erected by public subscription.'

She longed to return the pressure of his hand, but forced herself to disentangle her fingers in a casual manner. And then, as a slight breathlessness seemed to grip her, she had a strange premonition of coming events in which she would find herself softening towards him.

They left the Puppy Memorial and moved towards the fence guarding the drop at the edge of the grounds. Below them a path descended the steep hillside to disappear beneath the branches of the eucalyptus trees clinging with tangled roots to the precipitous banks. Beyond the treetops, stretching into the blue-mauve haze of distance, was the unforgettable panorama that never ceased to fill Robyn with awe.

She no longer had the desire to chatter, and although she was aware that he again stood very close to her she gazed towards the vastness of the undulating hills and valleys that merged in layers as they changed from coastal lowlands to the heights of the ranges. The sun had now disappeared, the last of its rays resting on the only distinct feature of the land, the nearby Table Top Mountain with its clustering growth encircling the flat summit like a bushy green necklace.

Turning westward, they faced a kaleidoscope of colour, the lower band of blood-red, jagged and broken by the almost black silhouette of treetops, chimneys and rooftops along the Toowoomba skyline. Flaming upward were crimson and vermilion streaks which changed to orange before fading to yellow, and then, merging with the remaining blue of the sky, the yellow turned to green.

The Queensland sunsets never ceased to fascinate Robyn, and this time, as she came out of the trance of watching the changing colours, she realised she was alone with Jonas on Picnic Point. Her former nervousness closed in again and she was about to suggest that Holly would be waiting for them, when she became aware of his lips brushing her ear.

'It's fantastic—and the colours seem to last for so long,' he murmured as though whispering in a church.

She quivered slightly at his touch, yet did her best to remain unmoved by his nearness. Her voice was calm as she explained, 'It's caused by the fine red dust rising from the planes of the desert out west. It hangs on the air unless there's a wind to blow it away.' She knew that his arm had slid about her waist, yet she seemed powerless to move.

They stood in silence, drinking in the vivid beauty that glowed over the shadowy landscape until Robyn looked up to stare above them. 'Sometimes the clouds are gorgeous—just like brilliant objects. Look, there's a pot of gold spilling silver—and there is a purple plough'——' She pointed upward, then dropped her hand and fell silent because she knew her voice held a tremor.

'Really?' Jonas made no attempt to examine the pot of gold, nor did he appear to be interested in the purple plough. The arm about her waist tightened and drew her closer to him until suddenly both arms were holding her against his body. His fingers beneath her chin tilted her face upward, and she trembled as his mouth closed over her own.

Her hands went to his shoulders in a feeble attempt to push him away, but as his kiss deepened to part her lips and reveal a rush of desire she found herself responding to the emotions that shook him. Her arms crept about his neck, and instead of the intended repulse her fingers clutched at him convulsively as she gave herself up to the tingling sensation that invaded her quivering body. At last she became aware that he was staring down into her upturned face, a set of grim lines etched about his mouth.

'You've been lying to me,' he accused quietly.

Robyn was puzzled. '*Lying?* What do you mean?'

'You've been trying to tell me you're an icicle—one who hates men—but a man-hater doesn't kiss like that. It means you're not really honest after all.'

Confused and lost for words, she stared at him speechlessly.

'You've just been playing hard to get,' he continued ruthlessly, 'but I can see that if you'd let yourself go you could be a hot little number.'

She stepped back, an angry flush covering her face. 'How dare you say such a thing? Why did you kiss me like that if you intended to insult me?'

Near tears, she slipped from his arms and fled towards the path that led down the hill. He was after her in a flash, his long legs taking him to her side before she could reach the first bend of the zigzag that twisted down into the gloom.

'Where the devil are you going?' he demanded angrily.

'I don't care where I go, so long as it's away from you.'

'Don't be silly—I didn't mean to insult you. It's not insulting to be appreciated as one who can respond with real passion. It's more of a compliment than anything else.'

She gave a small stamp of fury. 'I don't like to be referred to as a *hot little number*. It sounds so—so *cheap*!'

'Don't be prudish. You've had affairs, haven't you?'

She shook her head. 'Not really—apart from one that was a complete disaster—the one that made me hate all men.'

The sunset was fading and beneath the overhanging gum tree branches the path had become dark. His arms drew her towards him again, his hand pressing her head against his shoulder. 'Poor little Robyn,' he murmured. 'Personally I think you've taken whatever happened far too seriously. You should brush it under the mat, and instead of allowing it to warp your life just look on it as lesson number one.'

'I'd been doing that very nicely until a short time ago.'

'Are you telling me I stepped over your defences?' he asked in a surprisingly gentle tone. Again his arms were holding her a prisoner while his lips brushed a soft line from her brow to her cheeks, pausing in their path to touch her lids.

Somewhere at the back of her mind a small voice whispered warnings to fight against the almost overwhelming joy of the pressure of his body against her own; but instead of listening to it and heeding the fact that these moments would only lead to tears because he was merely amusing himself, she found herself eagerly waiting for his lips to reach her own. When they did her arms clung to him as ardently as before until at last, breathlessly, she dragged her mouth away and leaned trembling against his male strength.

And now will come a caustic remark, she thought bitterly.

But as they remained close together in the gathering darkness the silence between them was not broken until Jonas said, 'Holly will be wondering where we are. She expects me to bring you home for the evening meal.'

She laughed shakily. 'Well, that's a surprise! I expected you to say something quite different—something cutting, as usual.'

He ignored the remark and went on, 'The question of her move to New Zealand has been in her mind all day. She promised to give me her decision this evening and I think she'd like you to be there.'

'Ah, of course, I see it all. Revelation dawns upon me.' She began to laugh until she was in danger of becoming hysterical.

He grabbed her by the shoulders and shook her roughly. 'What the devil's got into you?'

'I *wondered* why you were being so nice instead of your usual sarcastic self—and now I *know*. You want me to persuade Holly to make the right decision for you and your plans.'

'*My plans?*' Jonas peered through the gloom, trying to read her face. 'What the hell are you talking about?'

'Haven't you a few plans tucked away, Jonas? Plans which involve assistance from Holly?'

'You mean financial assistance? Have you the temerity to suggest I'm looking for money from her? My oath, you've got a nerve!' His hands dropped from her shoulders where they had rested during the last few moments and he strode up the path.

It was lighter at the top with only a glimmer of pale orange remaining on the horizon. She followed him across the grass, almost running to keep up with him, and they drove back to Coolabah in silence.

As they walked in the door Holly greeted them with surprise. 'You're home already? I was sure you'd be up there for ages, so I made a casserole that could sit in the oven and wait till you came in. Weren't the colours marvellous this evening? I couldn't help thinking of my two dear ones up there, so close to all that magic beauty.'

Her two dear ones? Robyn was startled. Was Holly nursing romantic notions concerning Jonas and herself? If so she could forget it, otherwise she'd be heading for disappointment. She glanced at Jonas to see if he had noticed his aunt's remark, but the only indication lay in a grim line about his mouth—that same mouth which had so recently crushed her own in what she had imagined to be passion, but in reality had been merely part of a softening-up process, a form of persuasion to

coax her to aid and abet him in his plan. She drew a
sharp breath as she recalled the intensity of that last
kiss.

'We kept our feet on the ground,' Jonas told Holly
dryly.

'And we intend to keep them there,' added Robyn,
flashing a cold glance at Jonas.

The casseroles containing meat and vegetables were
put on the trolley and pushed towards the dining table.
Holly served the meal and they ate in silence until she
said to Robyn, 'Jonas is still trying to persuade me to
move over to New Zealand.'

Jonas patted his aunt's hand. 'I'm serious about it,
Aunt. I wish you'd realise it's for your own good.'

'And I wish I could be sure of that.' She sighed and
sent Robyn an expectant look as though waiting for her
comment.

Robyn thought for several moments, then, without
looking at Jonas, she said carefully, 'There's a very
important point to be given consideration. If you leave
here to live at Brightlands you'll be giving up your own
roof. Have you thought of that?'

Holly's eyes widened a little. '*No*—I haven't——'

Still without looking at Jonas, Robyn went on, 'I've
always understood that as one grows older one's own
roof isn't to be tossed aside. It's one's *own place*.'

'You're right—of course you're right,' Holly quavered
as this fact struck her for the first time. 'I've lived under
my own roof for so long I'd ceased to appreciate it.
George put this roof over my head,' she murmured,
looking upwards.

'Hell's bells, you're a great help!' Jonas snarled at
Robyn, fury glittering from behind half-closed lids. 'My
aunt can have her own roof over there as easily as she
can have it here. If she's not satisfied with the
Brightlands roof she can acquire one of her own by
buying a flat or a small house.'

'Where she'd feel most unsettled and not at all like

home,' Robyn cut in. 'No, I feel that to suddenly sell everything here and move over there would be a tremendous wrench for one of Holly's temperament. I fear it could be too much for her.'

His mouth gripped in an angry line as his voice became heavy with sarcasm. 'With your reputation for common sense I'm sure you're about to come up with a suggestion of some sort.'

'Yes—as a matter of fact I am.'

'No doubt it'll be clever and subtle,' he gritted.

'I don't know about that. Nor am I sure it'll tie in with your own particular plans.' The brown eyes sent him a direct look while her smile was full of innocence.

He glared at her from beneath drawn brows. 'Get on with it,' he rasped. 'Let's have this wonderful suggestion.'

Robyn drew a deep breath. She felt sure Jonas would be against it, and no doubt furious with her, but she also knew that if Holly couldn't think of this simple scheme for herself it had to be placed before her. She turned to her elderly neighbour and said,

'Well, instead of burning your boats by selling up here, why don't you go to Brightlands for a holiday? You could renew your acquaintances with your relatives—all these people who'll be so willing to rally to your assistance if you need them—and make up your mind after you've been there for a while. Don't let anyone *bully* you into doing something you might regret.'

'Meaning me?' Jonas demanded coldly.

'Meaning—let her have a look at the whole set-up first,' Robyn reasoned. 'It's ages since she's been there.'

'I believe it's a good idea,' Holly admitted slowly. 'Yes, I'd definitely consider going for a holiday of two or three months.'

'You could come back with me,' suggested Jonas.

Holly laughed. 'My dear Jonas, you're so impatient! You're leaving in a few days and I couldn't possibly be ready by then. Arrangements must be made for the house to be taken care of, and there are a few business matters to be seen to. I don't think I could go before early December.' She turned to Robyn. 'Will the Institute be closed for the year by then?'

Robyn nodded. 'Yes, my course will be finished.' Once again the problem of what she would do then rose before her, but she pushed it aside. It was a bridge to be crossed when she came to it.

'And there's another thing,' Holly went on, her voice quavering. 'I've become such a foolish inadequate old woman I couldn't possibly go all that way alone. I couldn't push my way through the crowds at the Brisbane airport, or lift my heavy suitcases on to a trolley—George used to do all that—and then there's sure to be all the humbug of customs at the other end.'

'Nonsense, Aunt!' Jonas's voice was crisp. 'Your travel agent can arrange for someone to do every single thing for you.'

But Holly shook her head. 'No, that's not good enough. I want someone to come with me.' Her blue eyes were filled with appeal as she turned to Robyn. 'Please, Robyn, will you take me across the Tasman?'

Robyn was startled. She looked from Holly to Jonas. The latter's face was a mask that revealed nothing and she guessed he waited to hear her refusal. Shaking her head, she said, 'I don't think Jonas would think that's a very good idea, Holly. I'm sorry.'

Holly sighed. 'Well, that's that. The thought was nice while it lasted and I wouldn't try to force you to do anything against your will. But of course if you won't come with me I won't go.'

Robyn was dismayed because she knew Holly well enough to understand she meant what she said. 'I'll take you to the airport and help you get on the plane,' she offered.

But Holly's mouth tightened into a line of determination. 'No, that's not good enough. Unless you come all the way *I shall not go*,' she declared.

CHAPTER FOUR

ROBYN turned troubled eyes upon Jonas. 'I'm sorry, I don't see what I can do.'

'Don't you? You can come with her—that's what you can do. Think it over.' His eyes glittered as he looked at her.

The suggestion that she should accompany Holly to New Zealand had taken Robyn by surprise. A holiday in New Zealand was something she had often dreamed about, but had known was well beyond her reach, and while one half of her longed to say yes in glad tones, the other half told her it was impossible.

Holly's voice cut into her thoughts. 'Perhaps you'll change your mind, dear. As Jonas says, give it a little thought.'

Robyn shook her head. 'Believe me, I'd love to come with you, Holly, but I couldn't afford it. It's as simple as that. My mother has overhead expenses for her new summer stock and my father has already financed me over the last three years. I couldn't possibly ask either of them for money——'

'I don't think you understand the situation,' Jonas interrupted, 'and my aunt is being rather slow to explain it. Your fare would be attended to, and you would also come as her paid companion. It would be more in the form of a working holiday.'

Robyn sent a quick glance towards Holly. 'Is this your idea, or is it the brainchild of Jonas?'

'It's my idea entirely,' Holly declared firmly. 'I've been waiting all day to ask you about it.'

Jonas's eyes seemed to bore into her. 'You must understand that my aunt doesn't want your assistance for nothing. She'd be employing you. Does that make a difference?'

Robyn hesitated. 'Well, yes, I suppose it does——'

'Then perhaps you could think about it and give me a definite answer before I leave on Monday.'

Robyn's eyes widened in slight dismay. *Monday*. She hadn't realised he would be leaving so soon and that when she returned from the Institute on Monday he would have flown across the Tasman. She would never see him again unless she went to New Zealand with Holly.

Strangely, the knowledge stirred something she had no wish to examine closely—something that was like a small pain darting within the region of her heart. What was the matter with her? she wondered crossly. Why should she care whether or not she saw him again? She hated him, didn't she?

Watching him covertly as one well-shaped hand raised his wine glass to his lips, she knew that actual hatred had never really been there, and that even her previous dislike for him had now mellowed—or had it been completely wiped away by those moments on Picnic Point? The memory of them brought a flush to her cheeks and she found herself unable to look at him.

Holly placed a hand on Robyn's arm. 'I know I'm stupid, but I don't want to go alone, besides, I feel sure I'd need your support when I got there.'

'Support? Why should you need support?' Jonas asked quietly.

'Well, it's your mother. You know what she's like. I'll be honest, Jonas. When looking back over the years I recall that one of the joys in coming to Australia lay in getting away from Flora. She was always so good at dominating me, and I don't like to be bossed. I know she means well——'

'You're forgetting she's living at Westshore, which is twelve or more miles from Brightlands.'

'And what about this—this Mrs Kerr? Is she like Flora, or is she a more easy going type of person?'

'Mrs Kerr runs the house very well. Barbara helps her.'

'*Barbara?* Is she living at Brightlands?'

'Yes.'

'Then that settles it. I won't go without Robyn.'

'Robyn will come with you,' he declared with confidence.

'How do you know I will?' Robyn flared at him, irritated by the fact that he was so sure of himself.

'You'll do it for Holly. It's as simple as that. The travel agency will arrange your flights from Brisbane to Auckland, and from Auckland to Hawke's Bay, where I'll meet you at the airport in Napier.'

It sounded so simple, yet her mind was in a whirl as it darted among the many things she must do. 'I'd have to get all my things out of the flat,' she exclaimed.

'Just pack them up and leave them in Coolabah,' said Holly. 'Your car can stay in the garage—I'll arrange for Mr Bridge to give it a run on his gardening days. Please say you'll come!'

Robyn was gripped by an inner excitement which she hoped was not obvious on her face. She'd go to New Zealand—she'd see Brightlands, the orchard and lands under cultivation, and suddenly the decision was not hard to make. 'Very well, I'll come with you, Holly,' she promised at last.

The next few days passed quickly, and during them Robyn saw very little of Jonas. She knew he took Holly to see the decorated shop windows and the competition home gardens which were a feature of the Carnival of Flowers week, and although she was invited to join them she was prevented from doing so by her assignments to be completed for the Institute. Nor did she see much of Sally, who was kept busy with rehearsals.

It was Friday afternoon before she saw Jonas again. He walked into the flat to find her surrounded by books and busily tapping on her portable typewriter. 'The Wolseley indicated you were working at home,' he said.

Not a word about having been given the use of the

garage, she noticed. No doubt being Holly's nephew as well as her guest he took it as his right, but he could have uttered a brief thank you. *Demanding*—that's what he was!

He went to the table and picked up a book. 'This is about music. I thought you were learning about painting.'

'We have to do what's known as an option study as an extra. It's looked upon as a valuable complement to our main course. I've taken History of Music for it because I can play the piano a little, but before I began it I knew next to nothing about theory.'

'Then it's useless suggesting you come with us to see the flowers in the churches. Actually, Holly sent me in to make sure you're coming with us to see the big parade tomorrow.'

Holly had sent him, she noticed. He hadn't come of his own accord. 'Yes, I'll come with you,' she said, hiding her disappointment by inserting a new page in the typewriter.

But disappointment was forgotten next day as they stood in the warm Queensland sun to watch the long line of spectacular floats that passed before them, each seeming to vie with its neighbour for beauty and originality. Every float told of months of planning and long hours of work by dedicated people, and the crowd roared its approval as the enthroned Carnival Queen and her princesses passed in triumph.

Robyn pointed to a large bird with outspread wings. 'That's the Institute's float. It's a phoenix rising from the flames. Don't you love its mortarboard cap?'

The procession was interspersed by bands, teams of marching girls who moved with precision and stared straight ahead as they ignored the antics of cavorting clowns. Cheers and applause rose on the air as a particular float or group caught the public's approval, but at last it all disappeared on its way to Queen's Park where each exhibit could be examined at leisure.

By that time Holly was showing signs of fatigue. She expressed the desire to go home because she was longing for a cup of tea, and a short time after Robyn had made it for her she was lying on the bed, remorseful for having dragged them from the festivities.

Holly's departure to the bedroom brought a tense silence between Robyn and Jonas. She was consumed by shyness, and was startled when he stood before her. 'You won't let her down, I hope,' he said. 'You'll definitely come to New Zealand?'

'I've said I will, haven't I?'

He gazed down into her face, his eyes holding an indefinable expression. His hands gripped her shoulders, drawing her towards him until, unresisting, she was in his arms. 'We stood like this on Picnic Point—remember?' His deep voice was suddenly low and vibrant, holding a huskiness she hadn't heard in it before.

She nodded against his shoulder. 'Of course I remember. I particularly remember your—reaction,' she added with a touch of bitterness.

'That's a memory I'm hoping to wipe out,' he murmured against her ear.

The pressure of his hand as it moved to the small of her back caused her to arch towards him. His head lowered, his lips nuzzled the lobe of her ear, then sought her mouth.

At first she accepted the kiss limply, until the urgency of his emotions began to send a hot flush over her body. Her throat tightened and the blood seemed to pound through her veins; and despite the memories of his reaction to her previous response at Picnic Point she again found herself clinging to him, her arms reaching up to entwine about his neck. Then, as his lips parted hers without effort, her own wanton emotions rose within her. She became conscious of an awakening desire that swept through her body as it answered the call of his need, until suddenly, although gently and firmly, Jonas put Robyn from him.

His voice was still husky as he said, 'This is something to be completed at a later date.'

She nodded without speaking, afraid to look too closely into his meaning. And if she was unaware that her eyes were like stars in a face that was radiant, she knew that Jonas had unlocked something that had been lying hidden deep within her heart. Nor would she allow herself to dwell upon the ecstasy of his kiss, the glorious feel of his arms embracing her as they pressed her closer and still closer to his body. *Later*, he had said. It was a matter to be completed later.

And then she became aware that Holly had entered the room after a shorter rest than usual, because she was unable to sleep. Jonas must have heard her movements, she realised, while she herself had had her head in the clouds. It accounted for the abrupt end to their embrace.

Holly, it seemed, was anxious for her to make a list of tasks that must be done before their departure, and as she wrote Robyn was dismayed to find her hand shaking. Concentration was difficult because she knew that Jonas watched her, an amused smile curving his firm lips, while the glances he sent her made her pulses quicken and the colour rush to her cheeks. Was he also thinking of *later*? she wondered.

Darkness had fallen when she went home. Jonas accompanied her in the moonlight and as they approached the flat he indicated the empty garage. 'Sally appears to be out,' he remarked.

'Yes. There's dancing in the street in town tonight, all part of the parade day activities. Rock bands and so forth——'

'Oh, I didn't know. It's not too late if you'd like to dance.'

She shook her head. 'No, I'm not in the mood for noise.'

Inside the flat he took her in his arms, kissing her long and deeply. Had *later* come now? she wondered wildly, her thoughts chaotic as his possessive hands dragged her thighs against his own and the surge of his desire stirred her own longing. Panic gripped her, giving her the strength to resist him before she yielded to the advances she felt sure were about to come.

'No, no—please—no——' she whispered breathlessly.

To her surprise Jonas released her immediately. She knew that his gaze raked every inch of her face, yet she was unable to meet his eyes until he tipped her chin and she was forced to look at him.

'You don't like my kisses?' he asked. 'You distrust me?'

'It's your mind I distrust—and the way it works concerning my character.'

'My reaction on Picnic Point still nagging at you? Then this will help you remember me until we meet at Napier.' He kissed her again, long and passionately, then left her abruptly.

As she watched his tall figure disappear into the gloom Robyn said faintly, 'Yes—in Napier. I'll be waiting—and longing—to see you in Napier.'

Later, as she lay in her bed and watched the stars beyond the moving curtain, she knew that she loved him. At the same time she told herself she was being ridiculous. How could she love a man who had spoken so harshly to her, and who held such a low opinion of her? Was she imagining this emotional state because he had the power to turn her heart into a pumping machine that had gone madly out of control? Was it his kiss, and her own avid longing for more, that had caused this state of mind? She'd be over it by the morning. Yes, definitely, she'd be sane by morning.

But when morning came she wasn't even remotely over it, and a further significant point hammering at her mind was the fact that she had never felt like this about

Gregory. Her emotional state concerning him had been totally different, and she now knew the main injury had been to her pride. *Pride?* Yet here she was, ready and willing to sink into the arms of a man who'd been suspicious of her honesty and blatantly insulting. What on earth was the matter with her? She must be *mad!*

Mercifully the next few weeks were so busy she was able to keep the image of Jonas in the background. September slid into October. The avenue of jacaranda trees in Ruthven Street broke out into clouds of misty blue-mauve blossoms, but Robyn hardly saw them as she attended to the many tasks to be done for Holly and herself.

The semester finished near the end of November, and with the break-up came the end of Robyn's three-year period of art studies at the Institute. By this time the image of Jonas had emerged from the shadows and was clearly before her mind, while the thought of seeing him again kept her bubbling with an inner excitement. Something to be finished *later*, he had said—and the time was approaching.

It was December when they flew to New Zealand. Everything went as Jonas had explained, the flight across the Tasman being smooth and easy. Three hours after leaving Brisbane they were banking over a mass of green hills edged by blue sea and white surf, and, as the wheels touched down, she knew a sense of unreality when she told herself she was in Auckland.

Their overnight motel was quiet, comfortable, and near the airport. The mini-bus which took them to it collected them next morning and drove them to the domestic airport. One hour after leaving Auckland their plane landed at Napier, and as it drew up on the tarmac near the buildings Robyn peered through the window. He was there, standing among a large group of people who waited behind the heavy netting barricade.

Her colour rose and her pulses began to race. She bent to take a grip on her hand luggage as well as the small bag at Holly's feet, and was thankful to have something to do with her hands. Moments later they were crossing the tarmac towards the waiting people. She longed to run towards the tall figure of Jonas, but forced herself to walk sedately while taking in deep breaths to calm her nerves.

The first shock came when she realised that Jonas hardly glanced at her. He embraced Holly warmly, but towards herself he sent only a casual nod. It was an anticlimax to the greeting she had built up in her mind, but after all, what else could she expect, especially as he was accompanied by his parents?

He introduced her to them. His father, Robert Ellingham, was a tall, quietly spoken man with grey hair and a firm jaw. Flora, his mother, from whom he had inherited his gold-flecked eyes, was a matronly woman who looked as if she would be capable of managing her own affairs as well as those of other people. Motherly, but bossy, Robyn thought, and this was confirmed as the older woman turned to her and spoke in a tone which indicated she expected no argument.

'Jonas has told us about you, my dear, and how very kind you've been to Holly, but really—she's so thin and pale! Well now, we're having lunch at our Westshore home and then I'll tell you my plans. I hope you'll both agree to them.'

Plans? What were her plans? Robyn wondered. She watched as Jonas and his father lifted their cases from the airport luggage trolley and placed them in the boot of a white Jaguar parked before the building. Moments later they were in it, but they drove only a short distance, because Westshore was a seafront suburb of Napier and quite close to the airport.

The house owned by the Ellinghams was in the more expensive price bracket. Fronted by wide sliding glass doors and large plate glass windows, it looked out towards grassy areas, the beach, and across the bay to the Port of Napier where cargo ships lay berthed. The sheltered patio was adorned by hanging plants and tubs filled with geraniums and petunias, and in these colourful surroundings they had lunch.

Robyn sat opposite Jonas, but not once did she manage to catch and hold his gaze. His glance flicked towards her, then slid away, and apart from a polite enquiry concerning the comfort of the trip he barely spoke to her. A vague worry began to gnaw at her, while the conviction that something was wrong grew stronger as the minutes passed. She felt bewildered and more than a little hurt, but she reasoned that whatever had upset him couldn't be her fault.

Towards the end of the meal Flora turned to him. 'Jonas dear, you're so good at making the coffee. Would you mind——?'

'Okay, Mother.' His tone was abrupt.

As he left the patio Holly sent an enquiring glance towards Flora. 'He seems very quiet. Is anything wrong?'

Flora lowered her voice. 'Take no notice. He'll get over it.'

'Bit of an upset at Brightlands,' Robert Ellingham put in.

Flora leaned forward. 'Barbara's left him,' she whispered.

Robyn felt herself go cold. *Barbara?* What did she mean to him?

Holly voiced the question for her. 'I remember Barbara. Are they engaged?'

Robert Ellingham frowned. 'No—although we've wondered if an engagement was in the air. She's been living in the house, helping Mrs Kerr and doing all his office work. He appears to be lost without her, and it's put him in a bad mood.'

Flora took on a determined air. 'Well now, that brings me to my plan.' She looked at Robyn. 'Robert and Holly haven't seen each other for years, so I've decided it would be nice for them to have a period together. Do you agree?'

'Yes, of course,' said Robyn, knowing this to be a fact.

'Also, I consider that Holly could do with a change of sea air. In short, I think Holly should stay here with us for a while. I'd like to get some good food into her, put more weight on her——'

'Yes, I understand,' Robyn nodded, wondering what she herself was expected to do. Fly home to Australia?

Jonas returned with the tray of coffee cups and as he placed it on the table his mother looked at him fondly. 'I'm just arranging for Holly to stay with us at Westshore,' she informed him.

'You're sure to be arranging something, Mother,' he said dryly. 'Does she agree?' He raised a dark brow in Holly's direction.

'Yes, I'd like that,' admitted Holly, her blue eyes thoughtful. 'But what about Robyn? I don't want to desert her.'

Flora warmed to her plan. 'As it happens Jonas needs help in the office at Brightlands.' She sent innocent eyes towards her son as she went on guilelessly. 'Didn't you tell me that Robyn's had clerical training, dear? Wouldn't it be possible for her to sort out some of the mess left by that girl Barbara?'

Jonas sent his mother an amused glance. 'There's no mess I can't cope with—at least not in my own office.'

'But you haven't the *time*, dear,' she persisted. 'Now don't upset things with arguments. I've planned for Holly to stay here with us, and for Robyn to go to Brightlands with you.' She turned to Robyn. 'Mrs Kerr will be there and you'll find plenty to do—so you won't object?'

'No, of course not, so long as it's all right with Holly.' She was slightly bewildered by the unexpected change in their arrangements, but knew she had no choice in the matter. In any case, with or without Holly, she was longing to see Brightlands.

'Good, then that's settled.' Flora's smile indicated her satisfaction. 'Jonas, take Holly's cases from your car.'

A short time later Robyn sat beside him in the Jaguar. They drove in silence as the white car purred over a bridge spanning a sea inlet that was busy with small craft, and then Westshore was left behind as they drove towards the Port of Napier. On their right a steep hillside was dotted with wooden houses which seemed to cling precariously, while on their left the bay sparkled between commercial buildings and large woolstores.

They drove round the foot of Bluff Hill, and as they skirted the town to head along the Parade bordered by colourful gardens and stately Norfolk pines Jonas gave a short apologetic laugh. 'I'm afraid Mother's inclined to be somewhat managing. She likes to make plans and to see them carried out at once.'

She smiled. 'I think you're *very* like her.'

He sent her a sharp glance. 'Are you trying to say you think I'm a bossy devil?'

'I didn't say that—but I think you also like to make plans and then see them put into action. Look at the way you've managed to get Holly here.'

'Are you regretting you've come with her?' he asked.

'Not yet.' The reply came warily before she said, 'I'm sorry if your mother's latest plan doesn't suit you, but there was nothing I could do about it. At least it'll be nice for Holly to have a short time with her brother.'

'I'll say this for Mother—her plans are usually good ones. Nor will sea air do Holly any harm. As for me— well, I *could* do with a little help in the office,' Jonas admitted reluctantly.

'But you don't want to take it from me,' she accused quietly.

'I don't like taking help from anyone.'

'Apparently you took help from Barbara. Tell me

about her.' *What does she mean to you?* was what she longed to ask.

'Barbara? She's really quite beautiful. Our fathers are old friends. She's one of the pickers who made me see I must have someone in the office. I managed quite well before taking on the extra land, but the time came when I found I couldn't be in two places at once. I couldn't be attending to clerical work in the office and at the same time be out in the fields while the ground was being prepared and the seeds sown. I like to see to things myself—it's a trait I happen to possess.'

'Or does it possess you? Surely you know that nobody does anything alone. Everything we do is for a reason which involves somebody else in some way.'

'I suppose that's right,' he agreed. 'I'll admit I thought I'd bought the extra land for cannery crops all by myself, but when I come to think of it I was able to do so only because circumstances forced the previous owner to sell it.'

She fell silent, touched by remorse as she recalled her earlier suspicions. How could she have thought his only interest in Holly lay in gaining financial assistance for the extra land? Loving him as she did, she now had enough faith in him to regard the suggestion as being quite ludicrous and not even remotely true. Plagued by guilt, she stared across the sea to where a long line of cliffs curved round the southern end of the bay.

Jonas followed her gaze to where the pale steep faces ended in broken rocks peeping above the sea. 'That's Cape Kidnappers,' he explained. 'In 1769 the Pacific explorer Captain James Cook had a spot of bother when he anchored the *Endeavour* out there. While he was busy trying to trade with the Maoris a young Tahitian member of the crew was seized and carried off in a canoe. Cook's men fired at the canoe and the lad was able to jump overboard and swim back to the ship.

'The incident caused Cook to name the place Cape Kidnappers, but long before that the Maoris had their own name for it. To them it was Mataupo Maui, or the fish-hook of Maui. According to their ancient legends it was the great fish-hook used by the young god when he fished up the North Island.'

Robyn laughed, 'That's what I call a good fish story!'

'Not only that—the fish-hook was made from the jawbone of his grandmother.'

'She must have been a giant of a grandmother!'

'It's said there were giants in the land during those days,' he told her gravely. 'In fact I'll show you one.'

'You will? Thank you. I'd love to see a giant,' she giggled.

They crossed bridges spanning the Tutaekuri and Ngaruroro rivers which were close to each other, then turned inland to pass through the township of Clive. Comfortable homes lay on either side of the tarsealed road, the acres between them being cultivated with an abundance of vegetable crops or fruit trees. Two large meat-killing and freezing works were passed before reaching the city of Hastings where they turned left towards the nearby township of Havelock North. The road was now a straight three-mile stretch, but still bordered by orchards, crops and commercial gardens.

Jonas nodded towards a large area of strawberries where pickers bent their backs between the long rows. 'You'll be tired of strawberries and cream by the time you're ready to go home.'

The words startled her. 'Go home? I've only just arrived! Are you suggesting I should start thinking about going home?'

He frowned. 'Of course not. Why must you take negative meanings out of casual remarks?' Irritation clipped his words but vanished as he said in a quieter tone, 'Don't mind me—I've had a lot on my mind lately.'

'Oh? Something to do with—staff problems?'

'Something like that,' he admitted gruffly.

Barbara, she thought. *Barbara's left him*, his mother had said.

However, he did not enlarge upon the subject of staff problems. Instead he asked, 'Have you seen the giant yet?'

'No. Where is he?' She stared about her.

'Keep looking,' he advised. 'He's there, all right.'

Robyn continued to gaze about her, then looked ahead to where the outline of the Havelock North hills rose beyond the town. 'Yes, I can see him—he's up there,' she exclaimed, her eyes following the clear silhouette of a large head and chest. 'He's lying on his back—'

'That's right. His name's Te Mata. He's waiting for his beloved. Waiting and waiting and waiting——'

'But she doesn't come?'

'Oh yes—at least he thinks she comes, but she takes on different forms. Maori legend says that Te Mata was a troublesome fellow with a great fondness for eating human flesh. When friends or relatives disappeared people knew the giant had caught them.'

'Why didn't they combine forces to get rid of him?' she asked.

'It's said they tried, but he was too strong for them. Their spears just bounced off him and he had only to reach out to grab another victim. At last the local chiefs decided to try strategy. They showed him a beautiful maiden, but kept her just out of reach by encircling her with fire. For days he watched her until——'

'Don't tell me—let me guess,' Robyn laughed. '—until he fell in love with her.'

'That's right, and it was exactly what the wily old chiefs had in mind. They commanded her to say she would marry him, but not until he'd first completed several Herculean tasks. He accomplished them all until he reached his final hurdle, which was to eat through the steep range of hills you see before you. But with his goal in sight he now became impatient to finish the job and snatch up the maiden. Do you see that gap behind his head?'

'A large square gap?'

'Yes. That's where he took one huge greedy bite, but it was too much for him and he choked until there was no breath left in him. Legend says he lay on his back and the hot summer sun welded him to the top of the range for all time.

'During the nights he thinks the maiden comes to bathe his body, but it's really the dew of evening settling upon him. He imagines she fans his cheek, but it's the west wind from the mountains, or perhaps a light breeze from the sea. At daybreak he feels her wrap a cool cloak about him, but it's only the early morning mists rising up from the plains or from the Tukituki river below him—and at times he feels her tears on his face, but of course it's the rain. Do you see that sharp point away to the left?'

Her eyes followed the outline of the hills. 'Yes, I can see it.' His description had surprised her, showing her a different Jonas.

'It's known as Te Mata Peak. I'm taking you up there.'

'You mean—now?'

'Yes, now. It'll give you a bird's eye view of the whole district before you reach Brightlands. You took me to Picnic Point, remember? I'll now return the compliment by taking you to the Peak.'

Robyn could find nothing to say as she sat staring straight ahead. *Did she remember?* How could she forget the hour at Picnic Point? The clear vision of herself in his arms was suddenly marred as once again she recalled his scathing comments concerning her honesty, and while she forgave him and tried to push resentment from her mind, the memory still had the power to hurt.

She gave a small sigh. No doubt the visit to the Peak would end in another disappointing anticlimax.

The sigh was not lost on Jonas. 'Is something wrong?' he asked.

She was startled. 'No. Why do you ask?'

'You're very quiet—almost as if you're unhappy.'

She gave a short laugh. 'I thought you were the one who seemed to be unhappy. I understand it's something to do with—with—Barbara.'

His jaw tightened. 'Do I hear an echo of Mother's chatter?'

Robyn remained silent, not wishing to say anything that could cause dissension in the family. A quick peep at his profile showed that his dark brows were drawn together as he stared ahead, and it needed little to tell her he was not amused.

Barbara's left him, his mother had said. What *did* Barbara mean to him? Again the question nagged at her, sending her spirits plummeting to the road beneath the car.

CHAPTER FIVE

ROBYN'S depression was shortlived as they drove through a residential area of attractive homes surrounded by trees and bright gardens. The road then ascended to wind through a less populated countryside of green hills and valleys where exotic houses were becoming established on the higher slopes.

'Do you like ultra-modern homes?' Jonas asked casually.

She hesitated, then answered carefully, 'I've never lived in one, but if given a choice I think I like a house to be old enough to have a homely atmosphere.'

'Brightlands is old by New Zealand standards,' he admitted. 'Sooner or later I hope to do a few alterations and give it a face-lift. I'll be interested to hear your ideas about it.'

'I wouldn't dream of pushing forward even the smallest idea. You might follow it and then be disappointed in it.'

'Barbara hasn't hesitated to say what she thinks should be done,' he mused with a light laugh.

'No doubt,' Robyn retorted rather more sharply than she intended. 'But then her position is different. She's been attending to your affairs——' And no doubt to the boss of Brightlands as well, she thought bitterly to herself. Something told her she was not going to like this—this Barbara person when she met her.

They drove between the high portals at the entrance to the Te Mata reserve, and from there the road followed the hilly contour as it snaked up towards the heights. They passed a building which Jonas said was Peak House Restaurant, and from there the road became narrow and even steeper as it wound round sharp corners. On one side rose a wall of grassy cliffs, while on the other side the land fell sharply to the lower levels.

At last they reached the parking area that was little more than a large turning bay. It was empty except for themselves. For a while they sat gazing at the extensive view, but when Jonas opened the door for her she was almost afraid to get out. She had never liked heights, and in one place the edge seemed to disappear.

He said, 'Come and see where the cliffs drop down to the river. Quite dramatic, really.'

She hung back, unwilling to go too close to the edge of the parking area, yet determined to keep her fear hidden from him. Her legs felt shaky, there was a strong breeze blowing, and a sudden blustering gust almost sent her off balance. Jonas caught her before she could fall, his arms holding her against him, the nearness of his body filling her with confidence.

'It's so windy—is the car brake on?' she asked nervously.

'Definitely hard on. If you'd rather not look at the drop——'

'You probably think I'm a fool. Of course I'll look at it.'

They moved to a point from which they could see where the cliff was scooped from beneath a protruding outcrop of limestone rocks before it fell down to the river. His arm was still about her shoulders as he indicated the blue ribbon flowing between its green banks. 'That's the Tukituki down there.' Then, after a pause, 'Do you feel better now? I know you were nervous.'

She nodded. 'Yes. I'll admit I felt scared, but I'm all right now. You've given me confidence.'

'Good. We'll take a walk up to the trig station at the top of the Peak. I think it says the height is something over thirteen hundred feet above sea level.'

He held her hand as they made their way up the steep

gravel path, the firmness of his grip giving her a feeling of security. But as her spirits rose she warned herself against taking too much out of the fact that he had held her close and was now holding her hand. They were merely polite gestures offered to allay her fears.

This seemed even more certain when they reached the top of the Peak and he released her hand abruptly. Pointing out various landmarks, he said, 'Do you see Napier's Bluff Hill? Follow the line of white surf round the coast and you'll come to it.' Then, indicating in another direction, 'That spread of roofing belongs to the cannery—those tall trees that stand up like spikes are Lombardy poplars. The district's full of them.'

It was indeed a vast panorama edged by the distant ocean horizon and to the west a backdrop of mountain ranges and farmlands. Below them the town of Havelock North nestled against the city of Hastings, the land surrounding both places squared off into market gardens and orchards.

'Can Brightlands be seen from here?' asked Robyn.

'No.' He pointed vaguely northward. 'It's in that direction but it's hidden by those humps of hills. The Tukituki flows along the eastern boundary. Come—it's time I took you home.'

Home. He was taking her home. The words had a lovely sound. She took a deep breath, closed her eyes and smiled as they echoed within her mind.

'Is something amusing you?' he asked.

Her eyes flew open. 'No. It's just that I'm feeling relaxed. Thank you for bringing me up to see the view.'

'It's different from the Picnic Point view.'

'Yes—in more ways than one.' On Picnic Point he'd kissed her, she recalled. Would he ever do so again?

Fifteen minutes later Robyn had her first sight of the Brightlands homestead. The car crossed an iron rail cattlestop to enter a drive bordered by rhododendrons and azaleas, their blossoms now spent, and as it stopped at the front door Jonas said, 'Welcome to Brightlands.'

She smiled at him. 'I feel as if I've been here before. It's all just as Holly described—white timbered walls, the two high gables, the upper balcony and lower veranda.' She got out of the car to gaze up at the higher windows. 'Upstairs there are four bedrooms and a small sunny room used for sewing. Two of the bedrooms have their own bathrooms.'

'That's right.' His eyes held a strange expression. 'And downstairs——?'

She closed her eyes as she tried to remember what Holly had said. 'On the left as you go in the front door there's a large lounge joined by folding doors to a dining room. On the right, there's an office and a library because your grandfather collected books. The kitchen and another bedroom are at the back.'

'Go on—what else? Don't tell me Holly didn't mention——'

'Oh yes—from the back door a path leads to a large fruit packing shed. It's always full of cases and cartons.'

'Right. That shed's really the heart of the place.' Jonas turned abruptly to take her case from the boot of the car. 'Only one bag, I notice. Does that mean you've no intention of making a prolonged stay?' His gaze was penetrating, demanding an answer.

'To be honest, I didn't know what to expect.'

He led her into the hall and towards the staircase at the end of it. The stained glass window above the stairs didn't surprise her, as Holly had told her about it, but now she paused to examine it. As she did so a woman came from the back regions of the house.

Jonas introduced them. 'Ah, there you are, Mrs Kerr. This is Miss Robyn Burnett.'

Mrs Kerr was tall, thin and auburn-haired. Her dark brown eyes swept an appraising glance over Robyn. 'Oh, so you're Mrs Hollingford's companion-help. I've put you in number five bedroom.'

Jonas frowned. 'Number five? Why have you put her in what used to be the sewing room, Mrs Kerr? Doesn't Miss Burnett warrant one of the usual guest rooms?'

The edge to his voice was not lost on Mrs Kerr. Her mouth thinned as she said, 'There's nothing wrong with number five, even if it used to be the sewing room. It's nice and sunny and near the bathroom. I thought it wise to keep the other rooms free in case your parents decide to stay while Mrs Hollingford's here. You know they often spend a few days here——'

'That still leaves two extra bedrooms,' he pointed out coldly.

Mrs Kerr's chin rose as she took in a deep breath. 'As it happens, I've decided to persuade Barbara to come back. Naturally she'll go into her usual room.'

'I've been given to believe she's nursing a sick mother,' Jonas said in a voice which indicated he really didn't believe this story at all.

'Actually, my sister's on the mend now,' Mrs Kerr admitted.

Robyn cut into the discussion. 'I've no wish to cause any upset in household arrangements,' she pleaded. 'I'm sure the sewing room will be just fine.' She felt embarrassed and was filled with a horrible suspicion that Mrs Kerr resented her presence.

Jonas seemed to sense her discomfort. He fixed Mrs Kerr with a stern eye and said, 'Robyn can choose for herself.' He picked up her suitcase and carried it upstairs.

But Robyn did not bother to look in Barbara's room. She walked straight into the sunny sewing room, which had everything she needed in the form of a bed, dressing-table and wardrobe. 'This is a dear little room!' she exclaimed. 'It even has a charming view over the tops of the fruit trees. I'd like to sleep in here if I may.'

Mrs Kerr sent Jonas a smile of triumph. 'I told you she'd be happy in here,' she declared quietly.

'You're right, as usual, Mrs Kerr.' He grinned at her

for a moment, then his tones became clipped as he said, 'I'm sure you'll agree that Barbara should stay with her mother until she's completely well. I'd be glad if you'd let her know she has indefinite leave. In fact I'll ring her myself——'

'Indefinite leave? What about the office work?' Mrs Kerr's voice rose. 'The pickers will be busy with the early plums and the first peaches soon. Who's going to do the wages book, may I ask? You can't expect me to do it.'

'Robyn will do it, Mrs Kerr, probably with one hand tied behind her back.'

'Will she, indeed?' snapped Mrs Kerr. 'Am I to understand that you're replacing my niece with this—with Miss Burnett?'

'That's the situation exactly, Mrs Kerr. It only goes to show that nobody's indispensable. Now I wonder if we could have a cup of tea? We'll have it in the office.'

Mrs Kerr's attitude subsided. 'Of course—at once, Mr Ellingham.' She hastened from the room without giving Robyn a glance.

Robyn stood with her back towards Jonas. She stared through the window but hardly saw the orchard. 'I think I have an enemy in this house,' she said quietly.

'Nonsense! Take no notice of her. If she makes you unhappy I want to hear about it. To be honest, I thought you were most diplomatic.' His arm went about her shoulders as he drew her towards him. 'I don't want you to be unhappy. I want your stay here to be something you'll remember always. Do you understand?'

She shook her head, then greatly daring because she felt so depressed, rested it against his shoulder. 'No— I'm afraid I don't understand. Nor do I understand you. One moment you're being nice to me, but the next minute you're looking at me as if I'm something you'd rather not see.'

His arm tightened about her. 'Surely it can't be as bad as that?'

'Can't it? How would *you* know?' She glared up at him and to her intense chagrin her eyes filled. 'I'm sorry to be such a fool,' she muttered, aware that her colour had risen.

'But a very nice little fool,' he murmured softly. He bent to kiss her lips, his arm tightening about her as he did so. 'You don't think there could be a reason for my attitude?'

'Reason? What reason? What have I done?'

'You've upset me. You've thrown me out of gear,' he retorted dryly. 'You've come into my life and altered my plans.'

'*I've* altered your plans? Of all the ridiculous rot— how could I possibly alter your plans? Surely you don't imagine I've influenced Holly in any way? The question of financing you has never been discussed—' She stopped, aghast at her own stupid runaway tongue.

His brow became thunderous as he grabbed her by the shoulders and switched her round to face him. 'Holly? *Finance me?* What the hell are you babbling about?' he demanded furiously.

She stared up at him mutely, unable to find words that would explain her indiscreet statement.

He shook her almost violently. 'Come on, out with it. What are you trying to say?'

Her eyes flashed angrily. 'Very well, I'll tell you. Just as you questioned *my* motives for helping Holly, I questioned *your* motives for persuading her to come to New Zealand. After all the talk of the extra land you'd taken up I guessed it was money you wanted from her.'

There now—it was out. She'd told him what she'd suspected. No doubt he'd be raving mad with her, but it didn't seem to matter any longer. The anticlimax of his cool greeting and the knowledge that Barbara had been living in the house had come as a shock which had plunged her to the depths of depression.

But instead of being infuriated Jonas snatched her to him and laughed above her head as he massaged her back with exploring fingers. Between chuckles that gurgled in his throat he said, 'You guessed, eh? What a bright girl you are, to be sure. What you don't seem to know is that even my aunt is unable to touch her own capital, because George left it securely tied up. She gets a good interest from it and that's all. But at least you were concerned on her behalf, which is something I appreciate.'

Robyn placed her hands on his chest and pushed him away with an angry gesture. 'I don't need your appreciation. Nor can I see how any of your plans could have been altered by me. As for coming into your life—don't worry, I'll be out of it as soon as possible.'

'Not too soon, I hope. At least not before you've sorted out my office. I'm afraid it's in rather a mess.'

The statement surprised her. 'Why should it be in a mess? Didn't—*Barbara*—have it under control?'

'I think it was beyond her. Her main job was picking,' he said as if that explained the situation.

'I presume you mean she was inexperienced in office work. Who took care of the accounts before Barbara?'

'Mother. She had everything at her fingertips. When she went to live at Westshore I kept them in order for a while, but I had so much to do outside I was too busy to give the office work sufficient attention. On this place the wages book has to be kept carefully, because there are so many casual and seasonal workers—men come to do the pruning, others to do the spraying, and when the fruit's ripe there are pickers and packers. Then there's the cultivating to be done for the cannery crops.'

She walked towards the door. 'You'd better let me have a look at this muddle in the office—and I'd like that cup of tea.'

'Right, but you've been warned. I'm afraid you'll find the desk jammed with accounts that should have been paid ages ago, all nicely jumbled with a mass of household accounts, and probably several cheques waiting to be banked.'

As they went down the stairs Mrs Kerr came from the kitchen. She carried a tray towards a door in the hall, but paused to speak to Jonas. 'I forgot to tell you—the man from the cannery rang to say they'd be starting on your pea crop any day or night now. Your peas are ahead of some of the other crops in the district.'

'Thank you, Mrs Kerr.' He took the tray from her and led the way into the office. 'The pea harvesters work twenty-four hours a day,' he explained to Robyn.

She poured the tea. 'You mean they work in the dark?'

'Yes. All through the night. Their machines have powerful lights and the peas won't wait before they become old.'

She looked about the office as she sipped her tea, and was assailed by the weird feeling of having been there before. It was a small room that opened out on to a side veranda. It was dominated by a large rolltop desk which was almost identical to George's desk at Coolabah, and there was also a cocktail cabinet with two easy chairs beside a small table. The walls held several bookshelves, and Robyn told herself it was only the similarity of the two offices that gave her the unreal feeling of being back in Toowoomba. However, she had to admit that the clutter in George's desk failed to compete with the mass of papers stuffed into the pigeonholes of the Brightlands desk. 'I'd better start on it at once,' she said.

'Not until you've finished your tea, and after that I intend to show you the packing shed. Then I think you should get unpacked and settled in your room. You're sure you don't mind being in the sewing room?'

'Not at all. I know Mrs Kerr would hate to see me in Barbara's room, and there's no point in antagonising her. And she's probably right when she says your parents and Holly are certain to arrive sooner or later.' She hesitated, then asked, 'Which is your room?'

'The one next to you.' He turned to face her. 'If you feel like visiting me just walk right in.'

She flushed. '*Visit* you—in your *room?* You must be joking!'

'I'm not, you know.' His face was serious.

'The day I visit a man in his room will be the day,' she said coldly. 'It also shows how little you think of me, otherwise you'd never suggest it.'

'I'm afraid you're away ahead of me,' Jonas commented calmly. 'I merely meant that you might want to speak to me privately at some time when the house is full, or after I've been away all day.'

'Oh. I thought you meant——' She stopped, feeling foolish.

'I know exactly what you thought I meant. Well, for whatever reason you come, the door's always open.'

A tap on the office door made them turn as Mrs Kerr walked into the room, a piece of paper in her hand. 'Excuse me, Mr Ellingham, this is a list of girls who've rung to say they'll be available for plum picking. I said you'd let them know about it.'

He frowned as he took it from her. 'I should have been given this list at least six days ago, Mrs Kerr.'

The woman flushed guiltily. 'I'm afraid it slipped into a recipe book in the kitchen. If *Barbara* had been here it wouldn't have gone astray.' She looked about her. 'I'm sorry there are no flowers in here. Barbara always kept the office so lovely with flowers—she took such care in arranging them.'

'Really? I hadn't noticed the lack of them,' retorted Jonas.

'And the ledger book—have you noticed her beautiful writing in the ledger book? Like copperplate, it is.'

'Yes, very neat. You may take the tray, Mrs Kerr. I'm taking Robyn out to see the packing shed.'

But Mrs Kerr was not yet finished on behalf of her niece. 'You know that Barbara did her best to please you, Mr Ellingham. Every single thing she did was for you.'

'I'm sure it was—when she got round to doing it,' he commented dryly with a glance at the desk. 'We'll go through the kitchen, if you don't mind, Mrs Kerr.'

'Of course not.' She smiled affably, pleased to note that the kitchen had been recognised as her special domain. 'Come to the kitchen any time you like,' she said with an unexpected show of friendliness towards Robyn.

Jonas led Robyn through to the back door which opened on to a large yard. It was sheltered by garages and an implement shed, and beyond it lay a vegetable garden where a man who appeared to be in his early fifties bent over young lettuce plants. A brick path ran through the garden towards the packing shed, and as they went along it Jonas paused to speak to the man.

'Hi there, Alf. Come and meet Miss Burnett. She'll be with us for a while. This is Alf Cody, Robyn.'

Alf straightened his back and wiped his hands on his trousers while sharp blue eyes took in every inch of Robyn's appearance. 'You're the young lady from Australia? The boss told me you were coming. I hope you'll be happy here—and that you'll stay for a good long time,' he added as an afterthought.

'Thank you, Alf,' she smiled, instinctively liking the man.

As they continued along the path Jonas said, 'Alf's not only the gardener, he's also the guardian of the shed. His living quarters are attached to the end of it. In fact he's my right-hand man, especially when the fruit picking's under way.'

'Where does Mrs Kerr sleep?' asked Robyn.

'She has her own bedroom and bathroom near the kitchen. I thought you knew all about the house,' he teased as he opened the door of the large shed.

As Robyn stepped inside to stand on the expanse of swept concrete her first impression was of strong cardboard cartons. Piles of them, flat and waiting to be folded into boxes, were stacked along the walls, while near them were more stacks, already boxed and waiting to be filled with fruit.

'Plums come first,' Jonas explained. 'We send them to the South Island because ours are earlier than their crops. They're all graded in this machine.' He led her towards a long contraption. 'The plums are rolled in at this end, and as they're eased along the centre belt the little ones emerge through the narrow gap of the opening while the larger ones come out as the space widens to let them through. It's an old machine but a good one.'

'I suppose the packers take them from these side trays?'

'That's right.' He moved towards a larger machine. 'Over here we have a more complicated grader for larger fruit like apples, peaches, pears and apricots. It gives accuracy in size and weight, and needs only minor adjustments for the different types of fruit.' He walked along the length of the modern machine, explaining and pointing out its various functions.

She tried to concentrate and to visualise its working as he showed her where the fruit travelled up the elevator to the sorting table, and from there to the spreader belt which sent it into the rows of the singulator until eventually it rolled out into the rotary packing tables. Eventually he said, 'You'll understand it better when you see it in action.'

'When will that be?'

'Before Christmas when we get started on the early peaches. By mid-January it'll be sorting early apples as well.'

'Mid-January—I'll be home by then,' said Robyn.

'You're sure about that?'

'At this moment I can't see a thing that'll stop me.'

'Then we'll have to find something, won't we? I can't allow you to disappear.'

She looked at him without speaking. These glib statements hinting that she could possibly mean something to him fell from his lips so easily. No doubt he was in the habit of making similar statements to—to Barbara.

As though wishing to change the subject he indicated numerous tubular steel trolleys standing in line near the wall. 'Those are wheeled packing stands to hold the cartons as they're being filled. You should see the speed of the girls as they snatch an apple in one hand and a wrapping tissue in the other. In fact there are apple-packing competitions.'

He led her to another area of the shed where he opened a heavy door. Turning on a switch outside the door, he said, 'This is the coolstore room. It's empty now, but soon the cartons of plums will be stacked against the walls. During the season fruit comes in and goes out all the time.'

Robyn peered beyond him into the empty coolstore. 'Does it become very cold?'

'It can be adjusted, but we keep it cold enough to act as a refrigerator. We don't allow it to reach freezing point, but it's too cold to stay in there for any length of time.' He closed the door, switched off the light, then led her outside through double doors which enabled a truck to be driven into the shed and parked near the coolstore. 'I'll show you the path to the river,' he said.

As they walked between the rows of trees she paused to examine the young fruit developing among the leaves. 'What are these trees?' she asked. 'I know I'm ignorant——'

'They're Gala apples, with Golden Delicious, Red Delicious and Granny Smith further over there. This is the pip fruit section. The stone fruit—peaches, nectarines and plums—are away to the left.' His arm waved vaguely to indicate direction.

Walking by his side among the stretching branches was idyllic. It was like being in another world, and although she longed to hold his hand she resisted the temptation. 'Would you believe I've never been in an orchard before this?' she asked.

'This is your first orchard? How does it feel?'

'It's so peaceful. Oh yes, I know the wind has dropped and I suppose that makes a difference, but to me the whole place has an eerie feeling of waiting for something to happen.' She sent him a sidelong glance. 'Go on, have a good laugh. I know you'll think I'm quite mad, but I could even imagine it in the shed.'

Surprisingly, he remained serious. 'No, you're not mad, and it *is* waiting for events to happen. In fact Brightlands plays a waiting game all the year round.'

'All the year round?' she queried. 'I don't understand. How do you mean?'

'These trees are waiting for their fruit to ripen. Those large bins near the shed are waiting to be filled, the grading machines are waiting for the bins to be wheeled into the shed. Even the cartons are waiting to be snatched up by the packers, who in turn have been waiting for the pickers, and so it goes on through the whole fruit-marketing cycle.'

'What about the boss of Brightlands? Does he also wait for something to happen?' She was unable to resist the question.

'Yes, as a matter of fact he also waits. He's waiting to learn the reaction of a certain person,' he said enigmatically.

'Oh?' Puzzled, Robyn waited expectantly for further explanation.

'It shouldn't take long,' was all he said.

She stared straight ahead, then sent him an oblique glance. What on earth was he talking about? she wondered. Did he mean he was waiting to see Barbara's reaction to her own presence at Brightlands? Or was he waiting to see a reaction of some sort coming from herself? It was impossible for her to follow his trend of thought and she had no intention of delving into the matter.

'Have you wished?' he asked unexpectedly.

'Wished?' The question surprised her. She shook her head. 'Wished for what? I don't know what you mean.'

'One always wishes when one does something for the first time—especially for an important event like going into an orchard.'

She laughed. 'Is that a fact? Then I must make a wish.'

'Close your eyes and I'll hold you steady while you do so.' His arms went about her as she leaned against him, her eyes closed. 'Now be very careful about your wish——'

It wasn't difficult to think of a wish, considering that all she longed for was to stay in his arms for ever. 'I've wished,' she said a little unsteadily.

'Good.' He tilted her chin. 'Then we'll seal it with a kiss. All wishes have to be sealed, otherwise they won't come true.'

Time stood still for Robyn as his lips rested lightly upon her own, and although she had a strong desire to entwine her arms about his neck she hesitated as she realised the kiss was only a light friendly caress and completely lacking in passion. When it came to an end she had a sudden conviction that he had patronised her, and that he looked upon her as a child in need of humouring.

Irritation filled her as they continued along the path towards the river, and as they stood on the raised bank to watch the swiftly flowing water she was only half interested in what he was saying.

'The Tukituki used to be a means of transport for the early settlers,' Jonas told her. 'People travelled up it in Maori canoes, but in those days the river was narrow and much deeper than it is now. Over the years there have been floods during winter, but Brightlands is safe on its higher ground. Some day I'll show you the picnic spots along the banks.'

She gave a light laugh. 'By the time you're ready to show me the picnic spots I'll probably be back in Australia. In any case I can always take a walk and find them myself,' she added coolly.

As they made their way back through the orchard Jones stepped away from her to take a closer look at a fruit-laden branch. She followed him, and had almost reached his side when she tripped over a pipe that lay hidden in the grass. A swift action enabled him to catch her before she fell, and although he held her against him for a moment he released her immediately.

'You're okay?' he asked. 'I should have warned you to watch out for the trickle irrigation pipes. The district is most fortunate in having underground water, so most of the market gardeners and orchardists have sunk artesian bores. This place has a network of waterpipes which are absolutely essential for good fruit.'

They walked without speaking for a while, but as they drew near the house the silence was broken by a girl's voice.

'Hi there, Jonas, I'm back! Just couldn't stay away——'

She came towards them, her figure tall and slim, her eyes a vivid green, her hair a flaming red. Even before Jonas introduced them Robyn guessed that this vision must be Barbara.

'Didn't your aunt phone you?' he asked in an amused tone.

'Oh yes—but you know what she's like. She babbled on with some nonsense about somebody else doing my work in the office, but I *know* you'll never replace *me*— at least, not after all we've been to each other.' The green eyes glowed like tree-shaded pools.

He gave a short laugh. 'Really? Exactly what have we been to each other, Barbara?' His voice was tolerant.

She took a few steps nearer and gazed up into his face. 'Haven't we been more than good friends?'

'I'd say we've held a good employer–employee relationship.'

'I'm sorry I had to dash off when Mother wasn't well, but I'm back now and ready to get on with the job.' Her eyes were wide with appeal as they gazed at him.

His mouth had become grim. 'I'm sorry, Barbara—I've arranged with Robyn to take over the office work.'

The green eyes flashed. *'Robyn?'* You mean this—this *art student*? What would *she* know about office work?' Her tone had become scathing.

'A little more than you do, I think, and that wouldn't be difficult. I think you fooled me, Barbara. You allowed me to imagine you knew what had to be done in the office.' He frowned thoughtfully. 'Or was it your aunt who declared you'd had experience of office work?'

'It was Aunt Jane, of course,' Barbara giggled. 'She wanted me inside because she thought she could get extra help from me.'

'But she knows she can get extra help when she needs it.'

'Dear Jonas, don't you understand? It was a matter of keeping the money in the family. Why should she get an outsider when I could do the extra work?'

'You should have been more honest with me. I didn't realise the accounts were in such a hell of a mess until my accountant began yelling at me for things that should have been taken to him ages ago. It's beyond me to understand what the hell you've been doing in that office——' His impatience was apparent.

'I've just *told* you—I helped Aunt Jane in the house.' She grinned at him and was quite unabashed by the admission.

'But you knew you were there to attend to the clerical work,' Jonas reminded her, his tone surprisingly calm.

Barbara shrugged. 'What did it matter where I was? I

was in *your* house, working for *you*.' She turned upon Robyn with sudden ferocity. 'And you've taken my job,' she accused angrily. 'I hope you're satisfied!'

'You're not exactly out of a job, Barbara,' Jonas assured her. 'Plum picking begins tomorrow and you can have your old job as one of the pickers. It'll take you right through the season until the end of the apple picking.'

Barbara flashed him a radiant smile. 'Oh, thank you, Jonas, I *knew* you wouldn't throw me out. And when this—this—when Robyn goes back to Australia I can have my old office job again?'

'That I very much doubt,' he commented quietly.

Robyn was suddenly tired of listening to the exchange between them. She was acutely aware of Barbara's thinly veiled insolence towards herself, and of the fact that Jonas appeared to be so bemused by the beauty of the girl he failed to notice her rudeness. There was no doubt about it, Robyn thought—Barbara was one of the most beautiful girls she had ever seen.

She touched Jonas on the arm. 'Excuse me, I'll leave you to finish your discussion. I'll go and unpack my suitcase.'

Barbara turned to her sharply. 'How long do you intend to stay?'

Robyn regarded her gravely, instinct telling her the reason for the question. 'I don't know. Probably for as long as Jonas needs me,' she said, sending the other girl a direct look.

Barbara's attitude switched to an unexpected friend-liness. 'We must see more of each other while you're here,' she declared sweetly. 'I'll take you out in my Mini. We'll visit the shops in Hastings and Napier, or we'll go down to the river to swim.'

Robyn wanted to laugh, but controlled her mirth. 'Thank you, but that won't be for a long time yet—at least not until I've cleared up that awful mess in the office.'

She knew her parting shot had been unnecessary, but it gave her much satisfaction to have had the last word. Nevertheless she felt depressed as she went towards the back door, passing a blue Austin Mini parked near it.

Mrs Kerr spoke to her as she entered the kitchen. 'Did you see Barbara? Isn't she beautiful?'

'Yes, she's lovely to look at,' agreed Robyn, her heart feeling like lead.

'They'll make a handsome couple,' Mrs Kerr said complacently.

Robyn paused to look at the housekeeper. 'Then they're really engaged to be married?'

'Of course they're engaged,' Mrs Kerr declared with conviction. 'It's just that they're keeping it a secret.'

'For what reason?' Robyn asked.

Mrs Kerr's thin shoulders rose in a slight shrug. 'What reason do you young people have for any of the things you do?'

Robyn made no answer, although the remark rang in her ears as she went upstairs. Even Jonas's father had said they'd been expecting an engagement, she recalled. *He appears to be lost without her*, Robert Ellingham had said.

She sighed as she placed underwear in drawers and hung dresses in the wardrobe. How long would they be there? she wondered as she closed the drawer on the last garment. Not for very long if she continued to be plagued by this present feeling of depression. After all, there was nothing to stop her from returning to Sydney.

The sound of the door opening startled her. She looked up to meet Barbara's eyes in the mirror. They glittered with hostility.

'I'm just checking to see that Jonas hasn't put you in *my* room,' she said coldly. 'I might have known he wouldn't do so,' she added with a note of satisfaction. 'And there's another thing—if you imagine for one moment that you're going to take my place in this house you're *very much mistaken*!'

And having made the situation clear, Barbara slammed the door.

CHAPTER SIX

ROBYN felt badly shaken after Barbara's outburst. Although it had been brief it had been unpleasant, but at least she knew where she stood with the fiery redhead. The main problem, she realised, lay in knowing how to cope with it. She sat on the edge of the bed until she knew she couldn't stay there any longer, and then, not at all keen to go downstairs, she forced herself to leave the room.

She reached the hall as Mrs Kerr pushed a laden trolley from the kitchen to the dining room. She offered to set the table, and had begun to place cutlery beside the table mats when Jonas came in with a bottle of chilled wine.

'We're celebrating tonight, Mrs Kerr,' he said. 'Find a couple of glasses for Alf and yourself.'

She flushed with pleasure. 'Oh, thank you, Mr Ellingham. I noticed you'd put wine in the fridge. I presume you're celebrating Barbara's return—I'm sorry she had to leave.'

He smiled affably at her. 'No, Mrs Kerr, we are *not* celebrating Barbara's return. We're celebrating Robyn's arrival and her first meal at Brightlands.' He popped a cork and began to pour the sparkling fluid into stemmed crystal wineglasses.

Mrs Kerr looked momentarily crestfallen, then her loyalties made a hasty move to the other camp as she turned to Robyn. 'My dear, I thought you looked very pale when you came downstairs. I hope my niece didn't upset you. I know she rushed upstairs and I also know her tongue can be sharp—but she doesn't *mean* what she says.'

Jonas looked surprised. 'Barbara went upstairs?

99

Why? I understood she'd taken all her belongings.'
He stared at Robyn, his hazel eyes demanding an
answer.

'She was making sure I hadn't been given her room.'
She gave a small shrug in an effort to make light of the
incident. At the same time she felt a warm inner glow
from the knowledge that he could see fit to celebrate
her arrival. It was something to hang on to—something
to treasure in her memory. She became aware that Mrs
Kerr was defending Barbara's dash upstairs.

'It's understandable,' the housekeeper was saying,
'the dear girl expects to be occupying her room again
before very long.' She served their meal, then left the
room carrying two glasses of wine for Alf and herself.

Jonas raised his glass in a toast to Robyn. 'To you,'
he said briefly, his eyes holding her gaze.

'Thank you.' She looked down at the food on her
plate. 'I'm afraid I'm not very hungry, yet I don't want
to offend her.'

He examined her critically. 'She's right—you really
are looking a bit strained. Did Barbara upset you?'

'It was nothing. I'll get over it.'

'I think you'd better tell me about it.'

'There's nothing much to tell except——' She
hesitated, then decided to be frank. 'She's afraid I'm
stepping into her position in this house. The situation
would be much easier to cope with if I knew more
about her exact position in this house.'

'Ah, I see.' He sent her a direct look. 'You think she's
my mistress? Come on, admit it.'

Robyn took a sip of wine. The thought of Barbara
being his mistress sent a stab of pain through her entire
being. 'It's possible,' she said at last, looking at him
across the rim of her glass.

'Yes, it's possible, but in your heart you don't really
believe it's true. Or do you?'

'Why shouldn't I believe it? She's very beautiful.' Let
him deny it, she prayed silently within herself. Please—

let him deny it. But the words she longed to hear didn't come.

'You don't believe it because you don't *want* to believe it,' he accused, his face unsmiling.

She flushed slightly and kept her eyes away from his penetrating observation. Had she been so transparent? Was her love for him written all over her face? Forcing herself to utter the words, she said, 'Why should it concern me whether or not she's your mistress? I've no wish to pry into your private life, but it'd be easier if you'd tell me a little about Barbara and her position here. It'd help me to understand my own position——'

'Very well, although there's not much to tell. Barbara's father is a successful businessman in Napier. He and Dad were at school together, and over the years they've kept in touch. Barbara always came with her parents when they visited Brightlands.'

'So you've known her for years. She must be like one of the family.' She tried to keep her voice casual.

'Not exactly. When she left school she spent periods in other towns, until one day she arrived home and declared she was tired of inside work. She wanted to be out of doors in the sunshine, and fruit picking during the season would suit her nicely. She came to Dad and asked for a job, and he put her on the staff.'

'Naturally,' murmured Robyn. 'The daughter of an old friend—how could he refuse?'

'She proved to be capable,' Jonas went on. 'In fact she's capable at doing most things—except controlling her own temper.'

'And clerical work,' Robyn reminded him.

'That part didn't come until later because Mother was here. However, the time came when my parents decided to live at Westshore and Mother was determined to see the house left in good hands. Barbara's mother heard about this and suggested that her widowed sister, Mrs Kerr, might be suitable as a housekeeper. Mother met Mrs Kerr and decided she'd be ideal. As usual she was right.'

Robyn watched his hands refilling their glasses. Well-shaped, tanned and strong, she had felt their strength, but instinct told her they could also be gentle. She dragged her concentration back to what he was saying.

'The accounts started to become a problem because I didn't have time to get at them,' he went on. 'When Mother was here it seemed so easy for her to keep them up to date, but when she went to Westshore they became too much for me, because there were periods when I was hardly in the house. Mrs Kerr then suggested that Barbara should be brought in to do them. I was assured she was capable of dealing with them, and took for granted that this was a fact. That's about all there is to it.'

Robyn looked at him searchingly. Was that indeed all there was to it? Had there been no emotional involvement with the daughter of his father's friend? She was feeling better. The meal, with its dessert, had been delicious, but she was aware that the wine was making her feel slightly uninhibited and in danger of talking too much. Throwing caution under the table, she leaned towards him. 'Will you be offended if I ask you a question?'

'Of course not. What would you like to know?'

'Your parents said there was an upset at Brightlands because Barbara had left you.'

'Correction. There was an upset because I discovered the state of the accounts. They're in one hell of a mess.'

'I can't help wondering—why did she leave you?'

His face became a mask. 'Why must women do any of the things they do? Barbara is unpredictable.'

'I see you're evading the question,' sighed Robyn. 'I'm sorry I asked. I know it's none of my business.'

'That was Barbara's trouble. She became curious about matters that weren't her concern. She wanted to

know how I'd spent every minute of my time at
Toowoomba, and when——' He stopped abruptly as
though realising he was about to say more than he
intended.

'Yes——? And when——?' she prompted.

'Oh well, what does it matter? You might as well
know every detail. I told her about you and she was
politely interested, but when I told her you were coming
here she became annoyed. She packed her bag and left,
saying her mother wasn't well and that she had to go
home.'

'You don't believe her mother was really ill?'

'I doubt it. Alf said he saw her mother shopping in
Hastings.' Jonas frowned thoughtfully. 'I can't understand why she became so annoyed. I told her about
Aunt's situation and the help you'd given her. I told her
about the Carnival of Flowers and its activities, but it
wasn't until she knew you were coming that she got
mad and left. She's so erratic I can't understand her.'

'I can. I can see the whole picture very clearly.'

'You can? Then perhaps you'll explain it to me.'

'It's simple. She's in love with you, of course. She
also knows that you love her but for some reason you
hesitate to make a commitment. She left you because
she hoped it would bring you to your senses. You'd
miss her—you'd go rushing after her to bring her back.'

His face had taken on a stony expression. 'What
makes you so sure I'm in love with Barbara?' he
demanded quietly.

'You've admitted she left because of my expected
arrival. And what did you say to me this very day? You
told me I'd upset you—that I'd come into your life and
altered your plans. I can only presume your plans
concerned Barbara.'

'Next you'll be saying that but for you I'd be
marrying Barbara.' His voice had become harsh.

'Well, I do appear to have thrown the proverbial
spanner into the works,' she pointed out. 'I'd better not

go swimming with her—she might hold my head under water.'

'You're joking, of course. You don't seriously believe Barbara would harm you?'

'I'm not so sure. I'll try to avoid giving her the chance. At least you've warned me that she's unpredictable.'

He scowled. 'If I thought Barbara would harm you I'd rip her up for packing paper!'

'That I'd be interested to see.' Her voice shook slightly because the topic of conversation was becoming a strain. He hadn't denied that he loved Barbara, she noticed, and although she waited for him to deny the suggestion the words did not come. She also knew there was a danger of tears flooding to her eyes, and unless she left his company soon she'd make a fool of herself.

Something of her inner emotion conveyed itself to him. He looked at her critically and said, 'You're pale. You must be tired.'

'Yes, I've had a long day. I'll go to bed soon, if you'll excuse me.' She did not add that the anticlimax of his cool greeting had also taken its toll.

'Perhaps you'd like a breath of fresh air on the upstairs balcony before turning in.' He piled dishes on the trolley Mrs Kerr had left beside the table, then pushed it out to the kitchen.

As she left the room her legs felt so shaky she stumbled and brushed against him. Surely it couldn't be the wine—no—it was utter weariness.

He noticed her unsteadiness and gripped her arm, holding her close to his side as they went upstairs. He led her to a door situated between the two front bedrooms and they stepped out into a night softly shadowed by a full moon. The air was still, the trees surrounding the lawn stood as dark shapes, the tallest elms being silhouetted against the sky. The perfume of roses in bloom wafted up from the garden below, filling the air with a heady sweetness and the night with magic.

She moved to the rail and took a deep breath. 'It's lovely,' she murmured. 'It's so—so romantic.' Again she felt unsteady on her feet, while a strange lightheadedness urged her to move closer to Jonas.

He stood beside her, the rough sleeve of his tweed jacket brushing against her arm and making her realise that here was a man with a difference. He was far removed from the smooth city type depicted by Gregory Blake, and now that she saw him in his own environment she knew he was very much a country man. She became painfully conscious of the magnetic attraction he held for her, and she also knew that if his arms went about her she would respond by clinging to him with the utmost wanton abandon while she lifted her face for his kisses.

But the moment did not come. His arms did not go about her, and with his hands resting lightly on the rail he began to reminisce. 'When I was a boy I used to sleep on this balcony,' he told her. 'One Christmas I was given a sleeping-bag. I used to bring it out here and lie gazing at the stars. They're not so bright when the moon's full, but you should see them during drought seasons on a dark cloudless night.'

'I'm sure they're beautiful,' she said, feeling frustrated. At that moment she wasn't at all interested in the stars. She just wanted to be held against him, but nothing seemed to be happening. Perhaps if she leaned her head against his shoulder—

'One night the rain came and I was drenched,' he went on. 'I caught a bad cold, so that put an end to sleeping outside.'

'Yes, it would.' Disappointment had her in its grip. Why didn't he kiss her? she wondered. He'd kissed her at Picnic Point—in the flat—at the Peak. Why did he hesitate now when the moonlight and the perfume gave everything such a dreamlike atmosphere? She drew a sharp breath, realising the answer was clear. He didn't

want to kiss her because he had Barbara on his mind. It
was as simple as that.

He waved an arm vaguely indicating the surrounding
land. 'During the early days of the province all this land
was part of a large sheep station which was later cut up
for closer settlement.' He paused to look down at her
while she gazed back at him. 'I shouldn't be rattling on
like this when you're almost asleep on your feet.'

'I'm not almost asleep!'

'Yes, you are, otherwise you wouldn't prop yourself
against my shoulder.'

Robyn straightened as if she'd been stung. 'I'm sorry.
Perhaps I am tired after all. Are you going to stay out
here?'

'Yes, for a while—but it's high time you were in bed.
I'll see you in the morning. Good night.'

'Good night.' It was almost as though she had been
dismissed. She made her way to her room and was soon
lying in the darkness. *Barbara.* Of course it was
Barbara. He was out there remembering the times they
had stood on the balcony together—the times he'd
kissed her in the moonlight. The scent of the roses
would bring it all back to him.

Tears of anger aimed at herself trickled down to soak
into the pillow. You stupid idiot, she chided herself
fiercely. Your course is clear. Get his office in order,
make sure Holly's okay and then get yourself home to
Sydney. And with that resolution firmly settled in her
mind she fell asleep.

Next morning she was awakened by the sound of
bangs which repeated themselves at intervals. She
sprang out of bed and went to the window, but could
see only the green treetops, their leaves shimmering
slightly in the soft morning breeze. Thoughts of the
office came to her mind. She showered, put on her
cream trousers and top, then went downstairs to find
that Jonas had left the house hours earlier.

Mrs Kerr appeared to be in a friendly mood as she

gave Robyn breakfast in the kitchen. 'The boss was on the phone early this morning,' she told her. 'Several of the pickers are already up the ladders. The plum trees are laden.'

'I thought I heard gunshots,' said Robyn.

'Oh, that'll be the bird scarers. Blackbirds and thrushes are the worst offenders. They'd get all the fruit if given the chance.' Mrs Kerr placed a set of scales on the bench. 'I'm baking this morning,' she explained. 'Mr and Mrs Ellingham are bringing Mrs Hollingford to see her old home. I'll make my fruit muffins and a cream sponge with strawberries for afternoon tea.'

'Would you like me to dust the lounge, Mrs Kerr?'

'Would you? It'd be such a help,' the housekeeper admitted gratefully. 'They won't be here until after lunch.'

Robyn left the kitchen and went to the office, where it took her only a few minutes to become utterly confused by names which had no meaning for her. There were so many accounts for the same commodities she was unable to decide whether some were being purchased continually, or were the victims of slow payments.

She frowned as she examined the recurring names. Jonas had not given her the impression of being one who would avoid his debts, and it was more likely that Barbara had failed to bring them to his notice, she decided.

She began a system of arranging the accounts into monthly piles and in sorting other papers according to their types. There were documents from the New Zealand Apple and Pear Marketing Board, and from the New Zealand Fruitgrowers Federation. There were glossy circulars advertising sprays, fertilisers, and an amazing array of orchard equipment which included hoists for fruit picking and the latest grading machines.

Scattered among the papers were household accounts, various receipts, power bills; cheque butts and bank statements. And by the time she had gone through the drawers as well as the pigeonholes she had an assortment of piles arranged across the office floor. This had become necessary because the small table near the window was unable to hold them in the required order.

It was lunch time before Jonas came in. He stood at the office door, watching her in silence before his voice made her aware of his presence. 'You were wearing that clinging cream outfit when I first saw you at Aunt's desk,' he drawled in a low voice. 'I must say it's nice to see you repeat the picture at my desk.'

'Except that there's no jewel casket—there are no opal earrings,' she pointed out dryly.

His jaw tightened. 'You never forget things, do you?'

'Things that concern my character are inclined to stick with me. That's what the memory's for—to remember.'

He was beside the desk in a couple of strides. 'You have absolutely nothing of a pleasant nature to remember?' he gritted.

She regretted the thrust about the earrings. It was petty to keep it in mind. 'Yes, there were other incidents that are nice to remember, but of course I realise *now* they were only—incidents.'

'What do you mean, you realise *now*?'

She spoke with as much dignity as she could muster, at the same time making a supreme effort to keep the bitterness from her voice. 'Surely it's perfectly clear. In Toowoomba I didn't know about Bar—I mean I didn't realise that despite your actions your mind was elsewhere. One could have thought that I, of all people, should have been warned——'

She dragged her eyes away from him. It was the first time she'd seen him in his working clothes and in some intangible way he seemed to take on a new personality. It was almost as though his masculinity was being flaunted at her more forcibly, and as if his male virility had been deliberately laid bare before her gaze. She found difficulty in keeping her eyes from straying towards the well-muscled legs beneath the khaki shorts, and from the tanned chest revealed by the unbuttoned khaki shirt.

His voice cut into her wayward thoughts. 'Warned against what?' he demanded.

'Oh—this and that. Meaningless incidents in particular,' she replied evasively.

'I think your emotions are in a tangle. They need sorting out, just as you're sorting these accounts.' Then, as though changing the subject, he looked at the piles of papers laid across the floor. 'You appear to be getting down to systematic work.'

'It's what I'm here for, isn't it?' She handed an account to him. 'Can you decipher this word? It occurs so often.'

He took the paper from her. 'That's copper oxychloride, one of the sprays used in the orchard. Spraying goes on at regular intervals because we have to cope with so many pests such as scale, mites, codlin moth, woolly aphids, pear slugs, leaf roller and a host of others. The sprays are divided into two classes—insecticides for the control of all insect pests, and fungicides for the prevention of fungus diseases.'

She handed another account to him. 'There are so many names that are foreign to me. What are these items?'

'Those are fertilisers. You'll soon become familiar with them. Now we'd better go to lunch, because Mrs Kerr takes a dim view of people who aren't there when the soufflé's put on the table,' he waited for her to precede him to the dining room. 'I hope you slept well on your first night at Brightlands?'

'Yes, very well, thank you,' she said, ignoring the memory of tears on the pillow. 'The guns—I mean the bird scarers woke me this morning.'

'After lunch I'll take you out to see them. You know

that Mother and Dad are bringing Aunt this afternoon?'

She was startled. 'Oh yes, I almost forgot. I promised to dust the lounge for Mrs Kerr.'

'When you've done that I'll show you the bird scarers, and then you won't imagine someone's trying to shoot you,' he said casually.

'You think I have reason to fear something like that?' she asked gravely, knowing in what direction his thoughts were heading.

'No. But you might *imagine* someone's out to get you.'

'I know you're laughing at me,' she accused. 'You think I'm stupid because I said Barbara might hold my head under if we went swimming. You probably think I'm pathetic——'

'Not at all. With girls like Barbara one can never tell.' His face remained grave as he lapsed into a thoughtful silence, and little more was said during the meal. Nor did they linger at the table, because Jonas appeared to be in a hurry to return to the packing shed, and Robyn was anxious to dust the lounge before the Ellinghams and Holly arrived.

Later when she carried a duster into the large room she hardly saw the comfortable suite with its covering of blue tapestry, or the polished mahogany furniture. Instead she was drawn irresistibly towards the grand piano at the far end of the room. The name Steinway caused her to draw a quick breath.

She longed to sit on the stool and run her fingers over the keys, but to do so would be fatal because tune after tune would run through her head and the lounge wouldn't be dusted before Jonas's parents arrived. Therefore, being very firm with herself, she set to work on the task of dusting polished surfaces, carefully lifting and wiping beneath Royal Doulton and delicate Dresden ornaments, and dusting round ornate vases that waited to be filled with large floral arrangements.

Not until the piano itself had been given a reverent wiping over with the soft cloth did she allow herself to sit on the stool and play a few of the pieces she had learnt during her option course at the Institute. She had expected the instrument to have a beautiful rich tone, and she was not disappointed when the bell-like treble and mellow bass notes filled the lounge.

Unexpected interruption came from the sound of Barbara's voice raised in anger as she swept into the room. 'My oath, you've got a nerve! Get away from there at once! Nobody plays that piano——'

'No? Why not?' Robyn sent her a brief glance of surprise but went on playing one of the recent popular tunes.

'Because it's Mrs Ellingham's piano. She doesn't allow anyone to *thump* on it.'

'I hope I'm not thumping,' Robyn forced herself to smile, refusing to become annoyed by Barbara's attitude. Her fingers continued to ripple over the keys without hesitation.

A show of temper began to make itself evident as Barbara took a step forward and tried to slam the lid down on Robyn's hands. But as she did so Jonas spoke from behind them.

'What the hell's the matter with you, Barbara?' he snapped.

'I'm merely protecting your mother's piano,' she declared defensively and with an angry glare at Robyn. 'Thump—thump—thump!'

'What damned rubbish! I was in the office and I heard Robyn playing. She has a beautiful touch. In any case, the piano's probably stiff and can do with a good thumping.'

But Barbara wasn't listening. She swung round and left the room, her face flaming with anger.

'The piano doesn't need loosening up,' Robyn assured Jonas. 'It's so easy to play and has a wonderful tone.' She looked up at him anxiously. 'Is it true that your mother dislikes it being touched? I wouldn't like to upset her.'

'Of course it isn't true. She'd be delighted to hear it being played. If you've any doubts about it you can ask her yourself this afternoon.' He looked at her searchingly. 'Why didn't you tell me you can play like that?'

She gave a small shrug. 'I didn't think you'd be interested. To be honest, most of my playing is by ear. A tune I like comes into my head and I seem to be able to find the notes on the piano.' She stood up. 'Are you ready to show me the bird scarers?'

'Yes—but first I want to show you a letter I'd like typed, and I want to make sure you can read my writing. I was drafting it in the office when I heard you playing. It was very pleasant.'

'Thank you.' Robyn felt a warm glow of gratification as she followed him across the hall.

But at the office door he was brought to an abrupt halt. She heard an oath of anger escape him and, peering beyond him, she saw that the neat piles of accounts which had been left in a row across the floor now lay in scattered disorder about the room.

Robyn broke the silence that gripped them. 'A great gust of wind, would you say? Or have they been kicked right and left by an angry foot?'

'Barbara wouldn't do this,' declared Jonas in a voice that was tense with anger. 'I know she's impulsive, but——' Words seemed to fail him as he stared at the papers spread over the carpet.

'You wouldn't suggest it was Mrs Kerr?' Robyn asked gently.

'That's ridiculous. I suppose you blame Barbara?'

She laughed. 'I'm not mentioning any names—I don't have to. In my mind the name of the culprit is quite clear, unless—unless it happened to be the person who was drafting a letter in the office,' she added teasingly.

'Are you suggesting that *I* did it?' He was wrathful.

'That's too childish for words. No, it's been done since I was in here, and I'm afraid it could only have been Barbara. My oath, I'll——'

'Please don't say a word to her,' pleaded Robyn. 'It'd be better to ignore the whole thing. It won't take long to get them into their piles again. Let me see the letter you've drafted.'

Later, when they went outside and walked beneath the trees, she realised the orchard was no longer silent. Ladders had been placed in various positions while gay laughter and chatter came from pickers who were almost hidden among the leafy branches. Glancing upward, Robyn noticed they all wore shoulder harness to which was clipped a canvas bag. It hung in front like an apron, and when it was filled the fruit was gently rolled from it into nearby bins. At intervals the bins were collected by a forklift tractor driven by Alf, who took them to the shed where the fruit was graded and packed.

Jonas peered into a bin. 'They're ready for picking, although they're still firm and not completely ripe,' he explained. 'Try this one.' He handed Robyn a plum that had ripened ahead of others. It was large, dark and juicy, and she ate it as they went towards a nearby bird-scarer which was set up on a box.

Jonas indicated a fat round container. 'This is filled with compressed natural gas,' he explained. 'There's a timing device connected to it, as well as a large barrel which explodes the gas at given intervals. When the barrel operates it's like the blast from a shotgun. I've got them dotted about the orchard. You'll notice they're on boxes so they won't be knocked over by the tractor.'

'Are they really effective?' she asked.

'I think the birds become used to them,' he admitted. 'Some orchardists employ a man to shoot birds, but I don't like that idea. I wouldn't like to see dozens of dead thrushes and blackbirds lying about the place. I'd rather lose a little fruit. I make a living—despite the birds.'

She liked him for not wanting to shoot the birds. He could be terse and abrupt, he could be cynical and arrogant, yet beneath it all he was kind. No wonder Holly referred to him as her *dear Jonas*.

His deep voice broke into her thoughts. 'It's time I returned to the packing shed. Don't worry about the mess on the office floor, I'd rather you typed the letter first and then Mother or Dad will post it on their way back to Westshore.'

'I'll do it at once so that you can sign it,' she offered.

'Good. Go back to the house by the path that runs between these trees. There won't be so many ladders to dodge because the plums seem to be slightly slower to ripen in this area.'

She left him and walked along the path he had indicated. She could see only one ladder, and as she approached it Barbara's voice called to her.

'Hi there—have some plums.'

Pausing beneath the tree, she looked up—and was suddenly pelted at close range by plums that struck her face and her head. The force of them on her eyes and nose hurt to such an extent that she screamed loudly as she covered her face with her hands. Then, staggering blindly from the tree and still keeping her eyes covered, she bumped into someone whose arms went about her.

Jonas's voice roared above her head. 'What the hell do you think you're doing?'

'I merely tossed her a few plums,' Barbara informed him coolly. 'It's not my fault if she couldn't catch them.'

'She—she deliberately hurled them at me,' Robyn sobbed against his shoulder. 'I can't open my eyes— they're full of tiny bits of leaf and dust——'

'Then you'd better go and wash them,' he advised, 'although I can hardly believe——'

Almost losing control, she stamped a foot in fury. *'Of course you wouldn't believe!'* she shouted angrily. Then, as she left him to stumble along the path, she heard the echo of Barbara's laughter.

CHAPTER SEVEN

ROBYN'S face stung, her top lip had become numb and her eyes watered as she made her way upstairs to the bathroom. The plums were being picked as they were turning colour, and when thrown with force they had the effect of being like small golf balls; yet the pain of their impact was less than the hurt caused by Jonas's seemingly casual attitude. Obviously, it was beyond him to believe his precious Barbara could perform such an act.

The mirror over the basin did not indicate much damage, although, peering into it, she could see bruises coming up on her cheekbone, mouth and brow. Copious tears had washed painful specks from her eyes, and after bathing them again she hurried down to the office. The Ellinghams and Holly would arrive soon, she thought, and she wanted the letter finished—otherwise Jonas would imagine she was putting on an act because a few plums had been thrown at her.

She found the portable typewriter which had been put away in its case, and although it was a long time since she had done any typing she finished the letter without errors. She then turned her attention to the accounts littering the floor, and was busily snatching them up when Mrs Kerr appeared in the doorway.

The housekeeper's raised brows reflected her disapproval. 'My goodness, you've got a funny way of working! I'll say this for Barbara—she was never in a mess with things all over the floor.'

Robyn compressed her lips and said nothing, while Mrs Kerr continued on her way to inspect the lounge.

Jonas came in a few minutes later. He glanced over the letter, nodded approval and admitted he was pleased with the way she'd set it out. 'I can see you've done this before,' he smiled as he signed it. 'Now then, let me look at your face. I think you said Barbara had deliberately pelted you.'

He drew her nearer the window and she stared up at him while he examined the areas round her lip, cheekbone and eye. She noticed his jaw tighten and saw a look of anger spring into his eyes.

'She seems to have got you at close range. I'll admit I really didn't believe you, but I can see there'd have to be force behind the plums that caused these bruises.'

'Why didn't you believe me?' she demanded bitterly. 'Are you suggesting I was telling lies—or was it because you didn't *want* to believe me?'

'I can only repeat I didn't believe Barbara would do such a thing. I've known her for so long, although lately I've tried to keep the relationship on an employer-employee basis.'

The statement surprised her. Was this as a protection to himself? she wondered, looking at him thoughtfully. Was he saying he'd been trying to avoid an emotional relationship with Barbara? And then, just as Barbara has got herself nicely into the house—I arrive. No wonder she's furious, Robyn thought.

She said, 'Personally I doubt that you've ever known her at all. However, it seems clear that you find it necessary to have her here, and that my arrival has disrupted the whole household. There's only one way to remedy the situation, and that'll be through my departure. And the sooner the better——'

'What confounded rubbish!' he declared angrily. 'I won't listen to such nonsense!'

'I can assure you it isn't nonsense, Jonas. I know you think I'm a fool—but I also know that while I'm here Barbara will continue to harass me. I don't have to take that sort of treatment from her—nor do I intend to do so.'

His jaw was tight. 'Okay, so what's your plan?'

'I'll put your office in order and I'll make sure Holly is well and happy. After that I'll quietly disappear.'

'Oh? To where, may I ask?'

'I'll go home, of course. I'll fly to Auckland and then go on to Sydney—wishing you and Barbara joy of each other.' Tears sprang into her eyes as she uttered the last words, but they remained unshed.

'You wouldn't be prepared to stand up to her?'

'No. I suppose it's because I'm a poor weak fool who's not very good at lashing out at people. I'm only a silly rabbit who buckles under and goes away to hide.'

'What you're admitting is that you run away. Do you intend to spend the rest of your life running away?'

'I—I might.' She turned away to avoid the intensity of his gaze which seemed to expose and lay her bare.

'Don't you know that life has to be faced?' Jonas pursued relentlessly. 'You don't climb over its problems by running away from them. If you do they only become worse.'

'I—I suppose you're right,' she admitted humbly.

'Well, at least that's something!'

'I mean, I know I'm a runaway. I ran from Sydney to Toowoomba. I ran from clerical work to art.'

'And you ran from the company of men to an elderly woman who was conveniently placed next door,' he pointed out shrewdly.

'Please don't suggest that I used Holly as a refuge, because that isn't true. I've become very fond of her and I want whatever is best for her.'

'Yes—well, we're not talking about Holly. We're talking about you and your habit of running away— a habit you're about to put into operation again,' he taunted.

'So? What if I am? There's nothing for me round here except—except unhappiness.'

He gripped her shoulders, his eyes holding an intense glow as they stared into her own. 'You're quite sure of that?'

But before Robyn could reply there were voices in the front hall. Jonas left her abruptly and went to greet his parents and aunt while she followed meekly.

Robyn was pleased to see Holly again and to find her looking happy and relaxed, but as the small woman came towards her she peered at her anxiously. 'My dear, what have you done to yourself?' she exclaimed. 'Flora, just look at Robyn's face!'

Robyn turned pink beneath their scrutiny, hesitating to recount what had happened in the presence of Jonas. She knew he was waiting to hear what she would say, but she also feared he would despise her for a miserable telltale. His sympathies would immediately revert to Barbara, whose little joke had been turned into a serious incident.

'It's nothing,' she said at last. 'I—I ran into something when I was in the orchard.'

'You probably bumped into the branch of a tree,' Flora assumed. 'It's so easy to turn quickly and collide with a low limb.'

'Yes, I'll have to be more careful in future,' Robyn agreed. She sent a quick glance towards Jonas, whose mask-like expression completely hid his thoughts, and then she became aware that Flora was asking her another question.

'Which room has Mrs Kerr given you, Robyn?'

'A dear little room, so sunny and quite close to the bathroom.'

Flora frowned. 'Don't tell me she's put you in the sewing room? Why didn't she put you in the middle room across the hall?'

'I—I understand it's to be kept for Barbara,' Robyn explained. This, after all, was the truth. It was the reason she herself had been given.

'Barbara? Mrs Kerr's keeping that room for *Barbara*?' Flora became indignant as she turned to Jonas. 'Would you mind explaining this situation to me? Why has Holly's friend been put in the sewing room while there are other empty bedrooms? It's almost an insult!' She glared at him, awaiting an answer.

Jonas sighed as though indicating the utmost patience. 'It's a complex situation, Mother. In a way it was to keep Mrs Kerr happy. You don't know her as I do. She's more than capable of leaving at a moment's notice if things don't suit her, and with picking about to begin I didn't want disruption in the house.'

'Well, I'll soon see about this,' Flora declared. 'Keep Mrs Kerr happy indeed!' she muttered as she left the room, grim purpose written all over her.

Robyn stole a glance at Jonas. Had his concern really been for Mrs Kerr? Or had he been endeavouring to keep Barbara happy? As usual his face told her nothing. She listened while he and Holly discussed some of the books on the shelves, and while she tried to put her mind to sorting the accounts she was painfully aware of his presence.

Flora returned within a few minutes, her eyes glittering with triumph as they flashed a command at Robyn. 'Come upstairs, my dear. I want to see you installed in a nicer room.' Then, as Robyn began to protest, 'Yes, yes, I know it's a dear little room, but after all it's the *sewing* room, and I'd prefer to see you in a *guest* room. If Barbara returns she can have the sewing room and that'll leave the two remaining rooms free for Holly and ourselves when we stay here at Christmas time.'

There was nothing more that Robyn could say. She stole a further glance at Jonas, then followed his mother upstairs. It took her only a short time to transfer her belongings to the room previously occupied by Barbara, and as she did so she felt a growing apprehension concerning the move. Would there be unpleasant repercussions when the others had gone? If there were, she told herself, she would have to find enough gumption to stand up to Barbara and her aunt.

Holly stood beside her as she arranged her toilet accessories on the dressing-table. 'This used to be my room,' she said as she looked at the white and rose furnishings. 'It's lovely to see you in it.'

Flora joined them, and as she stared at Robyn's face in the mirror she said in a quietly commanding tone, 'Now then, will you tell me what *really* happened to your face.'

Robyn's desire to go into the details was even less than it had been previously. 'Oh, it's nothing. As I told you before, it was an accident——'

Mrs Kerr's voice spoke from behind them. 'It was nothing of the sort.' She carried a cloth and began dusting a bookcase. 'You might as well know what happened, as you're sure to find out sooner or later. I'm afraid it was a deliberate attack by my niece. Yes, I mean it,' she admitted, glancing at the shocked expression on the faces of Holly and Flora. 'She pelted Robyn with hard plums because she's insanely jealous of her position in this house. Alf told me about it. He saw it happen when he was on his way to examine her bin. Mr Ellingham was there too.' She drew herself up and took a deep breath. 'There now, I feel better for having told you the truth about what happened.'

Her statement was greeted with shocked silence until Robyn, suddenly tired of the subject, pleaded, 'Please don't worry about it. It's over and done with, and my face isn't quite so sore now.'

'There's just one more thing to be said,' Mrs Kerr went on. 'I'm deeply sorry it happened. I had no idea my niece could be so vindictive. I hope you won't hold it against *me*.' She looked from Robyn to Flora.

'Of course not, Mrs Kerr,' Robyn assured her, then added generously, 'and please remember, if there's anything I can do to help you in the house you've only to ask.' She was more than happy to accept the olive branch offered by Mrs Kerr, as it meant there would be

an improved attitude between them for the remainder
of her stay at Brightlands.

Flora's eyes sparked as they held Mrs Kerr's gaze.
'Personally I consider Barbara's action disgraceful, but
if Robyn can forgive and forget the incident I suppose
there's little more to be said. However, when I think of
a guest at Brightlands being treated in such a
manner——'

'One of the *staff* is what I understand the young lady's
position to be,' Mrs Kerr cut in. 'May I suggest you
look on it as a tiff between members of the staff?'

Robyn laughed as she agreed with Mrs Kerr. 'Yes,
don't forget I'm the office girl, with plenty of sorting
out to do.'

The rest of the afternoon passed quietly. There was
little to be seen of Jonas and his father as the two men
had disappeared in the direction of the packing shed.
No doubt they were supervising the grading and
packing of the plums for the South Island, Robyn
thought. She found it easy to imagine Jonas's critical
eyes watching the swift hands of the packers as they
snatched the fruit from the revolving trays.

Flora Ellingham began to confer about household
matters with Mrs Kerr. 'We'll be staying here for a few
days at Christmas,' Robyn heard her say. 'I want you
to arrange for extra help in the kitchen. I shall make the
Christmas cake and the Christmas pudding. Yes, I'm
sure you can do them very well, Mrs Kerr, but I must
say I prefer my own recipes.' An indistinct mumble
could be heard coming from Mrs Kerr and then Flora
went on, 'Yes, I know it's often too hot for turkey and
Christmas pudding, but we always have the traditional
Yuletide dinner.'

Listening to the conversation, Robyn smiled to
herself. Jonas's mother, she realised, had not yet
relinquished her hold on the running of the Brightlands
homestead, nor did she appear to have any intention of
doing so in the near future. The girl who married Jonas

would have to contend with his mother's managing ways, but at least they were efficient and constructive.

During the afternoon it was Holly who monopolised Robyn's time and attention. She was anxious to seek a few of her old haunts, such as where the hammock used to hang, and after touring the garden they walked as far as the river. At last she paused to shake her head in bewilderment. 'It's not the same. Everything's changed since I was last here. Old trees have been cut out, new ones put in, the picnic spots on the riverbank are all different.'

Robyn took her arm comfortingly. 'One has to remember that nothing stays the same, Holly. You have to expect everything to be quite different.'

'Well, there's one thing that seems to be fairly consistent round this place, and that's the amount of work to be done. It grows more—never less,' Holly pointed out grimly. 'I can't help wondering if the girl who marries Jonas will have to take second place to the orchard.' She did not look at Robyn as she made the remark.

Robyn thought about it for a few moments before she said, 'I think the girl who—who loves Jonas—will understand the situation. She'll want to work beside him, rather than sit round waiting for his attentions.'

'I hoped you'd say something like that,' Holly admitted. 'I think I've guessed. You do love him, don't you?'

It was useless to deny it. 'Yes, I love him. Does it show so clearly? Don't tell me it's written all over my face!' The thought made Robyn cringe with embarrassment.

'Of course it doesn't show. It's just that I know you better than you think and I can sense the difference in you. Nothing would make me happier——'

Robyn gave a short mirthless laugh. 'Don't let your hopes soar, because he doesn't love me. He loves Barbara but hasn't wakened up to the fact yet.' There was a small catch in her voice as she tried to keep the bitterness from it.

'You mean that girl who threw the plums at you? What makes you so sure he loves her?'

'She's so beautiful, and he's known her for years—on top of which, various incidents have pointed that way. For one thing, he's hardly reprimanded her when she's shown how much my presence in the house infuriates her.'

'Ah, that's when you must prove your understanding of the acute situation, my dear. It's a case of the orchard coming first. You know they're working at speed because the fruit waits for no one. It has to be picked at a certain time and sent off to the market depot or to the cannery. To do this the pickers and packers are necessary, and Jonas doesn't want trouble among them.'

Robyn's eyes widened. 'Trouble? Are you saying I could cause trouble among the staff?'

'Only indirectly, dear. In Hawke's Bay where there are so many orchards, all with the fruit ripening at the same time, the position can be critical. All the orchardists are crying out for pickers and packers, and don't forget the busy time hasn't even begun yet. Next month will see early apples, nectarines and other varieties of peaches and plums ready for harvest.'

'So? I still can't see——'

'Workers are very independent these days,' Holly explained. 'Robert was telling me that if a picker or packer is told to leave the rest are more than capable of walking off the job. Do you understand what I'm saying?' Holly looked at her anxiously.

'No—not completely——'

'Barbara is a fast and capable picker who knows how to twist the fruit, especially the apples, which must have the little stem left on them. Robert says she's also very popular with the rest of the staff, mainly because she chats with them and makes them laugh. He says that some of them are probably looking upon her as the next mistress of Brightlands. Now you understand what I'm saying?'

'Yes. You're telling me that Jonas is in an awkward position and that it would be unwise for him to risk trouble because of a few small annoyances to me.' Holly's words had given Robyn a much wider view of problems in the orchard, and she could see that the most important factor was to get the fruit picked, packed, and away to the various destinations awaiting its arrival.

Holly continued to sing Jonas's praises. 'The dear boy has worked so hard,' she said. 'I offered to lend him money to help finance these new areas he's got planted in peas, beans and whatever else he's growing, but he refused politely, saying he had it all under control. Apparently he's used money his grandfather left him, so he's had to borrow only a small amount from the bank.'

Robyn said nothing, again feeling guilty as she recalled her earlier suspicions concerning the money Jonas would need for his extra land. And now Holly's own admission of having offered to lend it to him told her they had been unjust, while her thoughts doubting his motive had been unworthy.

Holly guided her towards the packing shed where they found Jonas and his father examining the plums as they rolled through the grader. There was very little chatter among the packers, whose concentration was intent as they transferred the graded plums into cartons which were then stacked in the coolstore room.

Jonas looked up as they entered the shed. He crossed the floor and took Robyn's arm, the firm touch of his fingers on her bare skin arousing disturbing sensations. 'Come into the office,' he commanded, then led her to a small area walled off from the rest of the shed by glassed partitions. 'This is the wages book,' he explained when they reached the desk. 'You'll see where they sign on at their time of arrival, and where they state their time of departure. You'll also notice that some aren't here for the full day. They're mothers with young children who can work only part-time.'

'I understand. You want these details recorded in the ledger that's in the house office.'

'Right. But see that the wages book is back in this office before the first morning pickers arrive.' His abrupt tone reminded her that she herself was merely one of the staff, and that she needn't expect any favours just because she was living in the house. And as this thought seeped into her mind his next words came as a shock. 'I'm taking you out this evening.'

'You are——?' It was an effort to conceal the delight that gripped her, and then her mind leapt to her wardrobe. What would she wear? Something formal or casual——? 'Where are we going?' she asked, being careful to keep the tremor of excitement from her voice.

'Nowhere really. Just along the road to see the cannery men harvesting the peas.'

'Oh——' *Peas*. She hoped her voice didn't betray the bitter disappointment of anticlimax.

'I thought you'd be interested,' said Jonas. 'The big pea-viners are really something to watch when they're at work.'

'I'm sure they are.' Her heart lifted. At least she'd be with him, short as the time would be.

An hour later they waved goodbye to Jonas's parents and Holly as they left to return to Westshore. The pickers and packers finished for the day, and Robyn took the wages book inside to transfer its details to the ledger in the house office.

When she returned it to the shed she collided with Jonas in the doorway. His hands gripped her arms to steady her, and for one long moment he stared down into her upturned face; then, abruptly, his hands dropped and he allowed her to pass to replace the wages book in the shed office.

'Mother reminded me about the Christmas tree,' he said. 'I was about to walk towards the riverbank to see if there's a young self-sown pine of suitable size. I don't want to be searching for one right on Christmas—I want to know exactly where to find it.' He strode along the path, then paused to look back. 'Aren't you coming with me?'

'I—I didn't know whether you wanted me to come——'

'There's no need to come if you're too tired,' he said gruffly.

'Of course I'm not too tired,' snapped Robyn, frustrated.

As they walked along the path he said, 'There's a large pine plantation not far from here. The seeds become wind-borne and the young trees spring up in odd places. Good soil and shelter from the poplars surrounding the orchard enable them to grow fast.'

They reached the edge of the property where several young pines had taken root, their soft dark needles covering branches that pushed bravely upward. Pressing a small cluster of needles to her face, Robyn breathed in a sweet muskiness that reminded her of warm fires on a wintry night. 'It seems a pity to cut them so soon,' she murmured. 'I hate to see a tree chopped down.'

'Some of them are too close together,' Jonas pointed out. 'They'd have to be thinned in any case—so make your choice.'

'My choice—— I don't understand.'

'You'll be doing the decorating of it. There's a box of tinsel streamers, glass baubles and coloured lights in a cupboard under the stairs.'

'*Christmas*—it's so *near*!' she wailed with sudden realisation. 'I want to buy a present for Holly and for—for——' She fell silent as she looked at him.

'And for your parents?' he asked, ignoring the fact that she could have meant himself.

She had, of course, meant Jonas, but she said,

'Fortunately I remembered to send gifts to Mother and Father before I left—and with strict instructions that they were not to be opened before Christmas Day.'

'Then who else did you have in mind, apart from Holly?'

'I'd like to find small gifts for your parents,' she informed him coolly. 'They've made me feel so welcome, and after all, I'm only a stranger to them.'

'Ah well, I'll have to give you an hour or so in Hastings. I'll be taking a load of plums to the depot tomorrow, and from there they'll go to markets all round the country. You may come with me—unless you object to riding in the truck.'

She smiled to herself. Object to the truck? She'd gladly ride in anything with him. 'Thank you—I'll be pleased to come,' was all she said, until a thought struck her. 'How does Mrs Kerr go to town? I presume she has her days off?'

'Of course—and then she goes by bus. It passes along this road in the morning and returns in the afternoon.' He shot a quick glance at her. 'I'll quite understand if you'd prefer the bus to the old truck.'

'No, thank you, I'd rather go in the truck with you.'

A cynical smile twisted his lips. 'Well, at least that's something. Some people refuse to ride in the truck. They look on it as a shabby old workhorse and insist on going in the Jaguar.'

'I presume you're referring to Barbara.'

'I haven't mentioned any names,' he retorted stiffly.

'You don't have to.' Then, unable to control a laugh, 'I didn't realise she'd reached the stage of dictating your means of transport when you take her out.'

His face remained unsmiling. 'I'll treat that remark with the contempt it deserves.'

By the time they went out the long summer evening was drawing to a close. A few brilliant red streaks lingered in the western sky above the ranges, but it was still light enough for Jonas to point out the extensive area of extra land he had purchased.

As they drove along the road he indicated a large field of dwarf beans. 'They're not yet ready,' he explained. 'They'll be harvested later by machines. Those long rows in the next field are dwarf tomatoes. I prefer to have them picked by hand as they ripen. That soft green fuzzy mass beyond the tomatoes is asparagus. It's now finished for the season. Can you see the sweet corn away in the distance?'

Robyn was straining her eyes to see the tall growth beyond the asparagus when she became aware that he was parking the truck on the wide grassy verge beside the road. He got out and opened a gate, then returned to the truck to sit and wait. 'Gates have to be twelve feet wide to allow the pea-viners in,' he explained.

'Where are they?' she asked, peering through the gloom at the large field, which appeared to be a solid mass of the crop.

He glanced at his watch. 'They should be here at any minute.'

'Did you plant all those peas?' she asked, wondering at the immensity of the task.

'Yes. The cannery people provide the type of seeds they want sown and I do the rest until they come to collect the peas. You'll notice they're not in rows because the seeds are just drilled into the ground from the seed-drill attached to the tractor. When the pea-viners arrive they'll move slowly over the crop. Flails in front of the machines will whip off the pods and flip them up into a long tank where they'll become podded—don't ask me how it's done—and then any vines, leaves and pods will go out the back and be returned to the field.' He glanced at his watch again. 'They should be here soon—they're usually punctual.'

Waiting with the darkness growing around them, they sat in silence with almost the width of the seat between them. And while Robyn was interested to learn the cycle of the pea crop, she was puzzled by Jonas's attitude towards herself. He had kissed her several times in Toowoomba, she recalled, but now, despite opportunity, he was obviously reluctant to do so. Why?

She frowned, searching in her mind for a reason, but continually coming up with the same answer. He didn't want to. It was as simple as that. In Toowoomba he had been on holiday, but now he was back at work and matters had to be put into their right perspective. There was no time for romance, and anyone silly enough to imagine that a situation which had been left off in Toowoomba would automatically resume again at Brightlands had better come to their senses. Not that there had been any definite situation, she admitted sadly to herself.

And there was his statement made in Toowoomba about *something to be completed at a later date*. What had he meant by those words? Vividly she recalled how—while holding her so closely—he had murmured them in her ear. At the time she had thought they concerned herself, but apparently that had not been the case. And now, the more she pondered the question the more curious she became, but before she could find the right words with which to question him he gave an exclamation of satisfaction.

'Ah, they're coming at last!'

The lights appearing in the distance were soon accompanied by the thump of diesel engines. They approached slowly, then turned into the open gateway, revealing themselves to be three massive hulks of complicated machinery driven by men who sat in high frontal cabs.

Fascinated, Robyn sat forward, her eyes following the progress of the strong headlights that made their way across the crop. And then she became aware that Jonas was watching her closely.

'You are interested in the pea harvesting after all,' he commented. 'When I first suggested it I almost imagined you seemed slightly crestfallen. I don't want to bore you too much with Brightlands' activities.'

'You couldn't do that,' she assured him quickly.

'Couldn't I? I haven't forgotten you're used to city life in Australia and that country life in New Zealand is vastly different. Although the place must seem very slow to you, I thought you'd be interested in seeing what goes on—while you're here.'

'While I'm here,' she repeated in dull tones. Apparently he didn't expect her to remain at Brightlands for any length of time. The knowledge depressed her, but she had been slowly learning to realise that this was the position and she must accept it.

But once again the question of what was to be finished later nagged at her mind, and this time she decided to satisfy her curiosity. 'Jonas, do you mind if I ask you a question? You needn't answer it if you don't want to.' She kept her eyes on the moving lights in the field of peas and tried to make her voice sound casual.

'Ask anything you wish.' His tone sounded suddenly guarded.

'Do you remember the afternoon of the Carnival of Flowers parade?' She longed to add, *you held me in your arms*—but found it impossible to utter the words.

'Of course I remember the parade. Is there anything special about it I should be recalling?'

'No, not about the parade—but afterwards——'

'We went home and had a cup of tea. Holly became very tired.'

She became frustrated. 'That's *all* you remember?'

'Not quite. I think I kissed you.'

'You *think*? Aren't you *sure*?' She might have guessed he'd forgotten the intensity of their embraces.

'And you threw an unpleasant memory of Picnic Point at me. You were quite bitter about it, if I remember correctly.'

'I had every right to be bitter,' she retorted.

'Would you mind telling me what all this is about? You said you have a question to ask me.'

Right—here goes, she decided, throwing discretion out into the night air. 'During that embrace which you appear to have forgotten so easily, you said there was something to be completed at a later date. What exactly did you mean by that?' There now, she'd brought it out into the open.

Jonas did not answer immediately. Instead he sat in silence for so long she began to wonder if he'd even heard the question.

'*Well*——?' she demanded at last.

He turned to face her. 'I'm afraid you'll have to be patient. I'm not yet ready to explain that remark.'

'Then you do remember it?'

'Of course. My memory's not completely void.'

'At least that's something,' Robyn retorted. Frustration again boiled within her, tears filled her eyes and she was thankful for the darkness. The moving lights in the field became a blur and the noise of the pea-viners drummed in her ears as they drew near to the roadside fence. 'I'd like to go home now,' she said in a small unsteady voice.

'Okay.' He started the motor of the truck. 'I'm afraid the pea harvesters must have been boring for you.'

'*Boring?* Of course they haven't been boring. *Nothing* about Brightlands is boring for me. What *does* bore me is when a person makes enigmatical remarks that I *know* concern me, and then refuses to explain what he means.'

'Poor little Robyn, you've had an exhausting day,' he smiled.

'You can say *that* again! I've had the work in the office kicked over the floor—I've been attacked by hard plums—or don't you *remember*?' she finished bitterly.

Ignoring her outburst, he asked casually, 'You like Brightlands?'

'Yes—very much,' she admitted, regaining her self-control.

'You don't consider it to be a place of non-stop

labour where workers are driven by the whip of a slavedriver?'

'No. Even a slavedriver can show reason and common sense if he can discover his own particular form of relaxation.'

'Hmm. I'll have to see what I can find by way of diversion.'

And that was all she would ever be to him, she realised sadly. A diversion, a momentary distraction from the routine of his daily life. Had Barbara also discovered herself to be nothing more than a form of amusement? No wonder she'd been engulfed by apprehension when her position in the house had been usurped by another person. No wonder she'd foamed with fury when that person had been brought in by Jonas himself.

Barbara could be unpredictable, Jonas had admitted, but to Robyn that was an understatement, as she suspected that Barbara could also be dangerous. The red-haired girl would fight for the man she intended to have, using any weapon that came to her hand, whereas she herself was more likely to run away.

Well, there's your answer, she told herself as she gazed at the truck lights picking out the road ahead. If you want this man you'll have to stand up and fight for him. But the next moment she quailed at the thought. Fight? Against Barbara? You've got to be joking!

CHAPTER EIGHT

THE house was in darkness when they returned. Mrs Kerr appeared to have retired and there was no sign of Alf. Jonas led the way into the kitchen. 'Coffee?' he asked, then without waiting for her to reply he filled and switched on the electric kettle.

Robyn's thoughts went to the men working along the road. 'Do you take tea or coffee to the pea harvesters?' she asked.

'No. I took it to them last year and the year before that, but each time they assured me they were self-sufficient. They carry flasks and food, and prefer to stop when it suits them. You can ask them about their midnight meals if they come to the staff Christmas party. They always get an invitation.'

Robyn's face showed her surprise. It was the first she'd heard of a Christmas party.

'It's usually held during the evening of the last payday before Christmas when a bonus is put into their pay envelopes,' Jonas went on. 'Pickers and packers bring their husbands or boy-friends. An electrician puts coloured lights in the hall where they dance, and a caterer from Hastings attends to the supper. Mrs Kerr is then free to enjoy herself with the rest.'

She sipped her coffee thoughtfully. 'You're very kind to your staff. I hope they appreciate it.'

He gave a small shrug. 'Mother thinks I'm mad, but I like to look after them. I prefer to think they'll want to come back next season. They're a good crowd and they work well.'

She stared unseeingly at the pattern of entwining leaves on her coffee mug. Next season—what would she be doing next season? She wouldn't be here, that was for sure.

'Is your coffee all right?' he asked. 'I gave you that mug instead of a heavy one. Somehow I thought you'd like that one.'

She raised surprised eyes to his face. As usual it was unsmiling. 'You did? Why?'

'Because I can sense you prefer bone china to pottery. You'd rather have refinement than homespun.'

'I suppose you're right, but how did you guess?'

'Let's just say I'm getting to know you.'

She flashed him a look of apprehension. 'Does that mean I'm—transparent?'

'Only sometimes,' he returned enigmatically and still without any trace of a smile.

Half an hour later Robyn was in bed, and despite the day's emotional stress she was soon sleeping soundly. Next morning she made a fresh start in the office, and when Jonas came in for lunch she handed him several cheques to be banked as well as a bundle of overdue accounts to be paid.

He took them from her, glancing through them with raised brows, then frowning with annoyance at their neglect. 'My accountant will attend to them,' he said in clipped tones, 'but thank you for digging them up. By the way, I'll be leaving for town at three o'clock, so be at the packing shed by then.'

It was an order, but she nodded, smiling because she was so happy to be going with him. 'I'll be there,' she promised.

Five minutes to three found her making her way to the packing shed, the knife-pleated skirt of her casual yellow and white silk dress swinging as she walked along the path. Glancing at the tall ladders, she noticed that most of the pickers were still busy at the plum trees, although a few had been moved to the early peaches which were now ripening. She also knew that interested eyes peeped through the leaves at her, because the story of Barbara and the plums had spread through the shed.

At the packing shed she found the truck parked right inside the wide doors beside the coolstore, and while Alf carried cartons and cases from the chilly interior, Jonas arranged them on the back of the truck.

'That's the lot, boss,' said Alf. He closed the heavy door of the coolstore and switched off the light. 'It's very wintry in there,' he remarked to Robyn. 'Definitely not the best place to spend any length of time, especially if you're wearing something thin like that pretty dress. Do you mind if I say how nice you look?' His eyes swept her from head to foot.

Jonas stared down at her from the tray of the truck. 'You look far too smart to be going out in this old faithful. Actually, the truck doesn't go well unless the passengers are wearing ancient jeans. It splutters with embarrassment.'

Robyn smiled up at him. 'I'm dressed for the driver—not for the vehicle.' The words were spoken unthinkingly.

'Let's go, then,' he returned dryly, and she was annoyed with herself for having made such a revealing type of remark.

There was a companionable silence between them as they drove along the road where orchards, vineyards and market gardens lay on either side. These areas were soon replaced by the comfortable homes of Havelock North, and after driving through its township they passed more orchards and commercial gardens on the road to Hastings.

While on this straight stretch Robyn twisted round to stare behind them, her eyes seeking the outline of the hills.

'He's still there,' grinned Jonas, reading her thoughts. 'I know you're looking at old Te Mata. The poor fellow's still waiting for his beloved to turn up.'

'Perhaps his beloved's waiting for him to *wake* up,'

she retorted a little tartly, then immediately regretted the words.

'Perhaps,' he agreed gravely. 'Some men *are* irritatingly slow.'

He stopped the truck at the eastern end of the Hastings shopping area. 'You'll find it's mainly one long street of shops so you won't get lost,' he told her. 'There's a clock tower near the centre of it.' I'll meet you there at four-thirty. Oh, by the way——' he put his hand in a breast pocket of his jacket and drew out a small envelope, 'this is your first Brightlands pay envelope.'

Embarrassed, she went pink. 'I can't take that—I haven't done anything to earn it.'

'Nonsense. Isn't the hassle of bringing Holly across the Tasman worth something—to say nothing of sorting out that mess in the office? Nor am I accustomed to staff refusing their wages.'

'Well, thank you,' she said stiffly and knowing it was useless to argue. Besides, his last remark had hurt. *Staff*—that was all she was to him and the sooner that fact became fixed in her mind the easier it would be for her.

As the truck drew away to some place that dealt with fruit she was overwhelmed by loneliness; but the forlorn feeling soon left her as she made her way towards the shops. Shopping in Hastings, she soon discovered, was easy, because each place seemed to be crammed with Christmas gifts of every type, the greatest difficulty lying in deciding what to buy.

Browsing from one shop to another, she eventually bought gifts for Holly, Mrs Kerr, Alf and Jonas's parents—but for Jonas himself she could see nothing that satisfied her. And then the problem was solved as she gazed into a shop selling art materials. Of course, that was it! She had the answer in her own two hands. She'd do a sketch of Brightlands similar to the one she had done of Coolabah. Mentally she went over the materials she had brought with her. Ink was all she needed to make it a pen and wash.

She went into the shop and was delighted to discover she could buy an attractive ready-made freme, complete with glass, mount and backing. She also purchased a block of good quality watercolour paper because she knew the block she had brought with her was too small to fit the mount. Then, satisfied, she left the shop and made her way back to the clock tower.

When Jonas arrived he took the heaviest of the parcels from her. 'What on earth have you been buying?' he exclaimed.

'Oh, this and that,' she replied evasively. 'I think I'd like to carry it myself. It's rather fragile, despite its weight.'

'Don't worry, I won't swing it at anyone, though how anything so heavy could be fragile is beyond me to understand.'

Robyn gave in, knowing he would never allow her to carry the parcel to where the truck was parked, therefore, in an effort to steer his attention away from it, she asked, 'Did you do everything you had planned?'

'Yes. I took the fruit to the depot, went to the bank and visited my accountant. For heaven's sake, what have you been buying? It's really quite heavy.'

'Good quality watercolour paper is always heavy,' she prevaricated lightly, hoping he wouldn't guess the parcel also contained a frame and glass.

'You must have bought a ton of it,' he remarked.

Robyn was relieved when the parcel was safely in the cab of the truck, despite Jonas's suggestion that it should go on the back. Then, to avoid further discussion concerning it, she said, 'The long straight shopping area of Hastings reminded me a little of Toowoomba.'

'Yes, there's a similarity. Did you know there's also an affinity of some sort between the two places? Toowoomba's Carnival of Flowers Queen is given a trip to Hastings as part of her prize. She comes at Easter when the Highland Games are on. Strangely, both cities are the centre of food-growing areas—Hastings with its fruit and vegetables, Toowoomba with its grain-growing.'

When they reached home Jonas carried the rectangular parcel upstairs for her. He placed it on the bed, then stepped back to stare at it speculatively. 'I'd be interested to see watercolour paper that weighs so heavily. When are you going to open it?'

'Not just now,' she said hastily. 'I—I have other things to do first——'

'You mean you're not going to show it to me?' His voice was cool.

'No, not at present—perhaps later.' If he saw the frame and glass he would be sure to guess she intended doing a painting, perhaps for himself, and it would take all the surprise from the Christmas present.

'You're making me curious. Suppose I decide to have a look at it for myself?' he teased, taking a step towards the bed, his hand outstretched towards the parcel.

Robyn became agitated. 'Don't you dare touch it!'

He laughed easily. 'Why not?'

'Because it's mine, that's why. It's private, and you've no right to open it.' Springing forward, she slapped the hand that was already on the parcel, then made an attempt to drag his arm away, but found herself swung round to face him.

'You slapped the boss!' he gritted, glaring at her.

'So what?' she retorted, returning his glare. 'Obviously it's the most important thing in the world to you—*to be the boss*. And because you're the boss you think you can order anyone to do anything. Nobody's allowed their own tiny atom of privacy!'

His jaw became taut. 'Is that what you really think?'

'If you want me to be honest—yes, it is.'

'So I'm the original overbearing male chauvinist pig, eh?'

'You said it, I didn't,' she retorted.

'But it's what you *think*.'

'I'll say this—it's the image you seem determined to present to the world.'

'And you don't like it?' The question came softly.

'Like it? Why should I care, unless it affects me personally?' She was careful to avoid his eyes, which seemed to be glinting at her with a special kind of interest.

'In the meantime you've decided to keep clear of my domineering ways.' A short laugh escaped him as, unexpectedly, he snatched her to him, his arms almost crushing the breath out of her as he swept her against his tall muscular length. His hard mouth sought her lips in a manner that was almost brutal with its sensuality, and which hurt the bruises she had received the previous day.

And while she longed to respond with arms that clung to him, common sense prevailed. This was not a kiss of love, she told herself. It wasn't the sort of kiss she craved for. It was merely a form of domination, and she was being chastised for having dared to utter anything that could be construed as criticism. It was an effort, but she forced herself to remain passive in his arms.

At last Jonas dragged his lips from her mouth and without releasing her stared down into her face. 'You're pretending to be cold,' he jeered. 'You can't fool me.'

She returned his gaze, hoping that the beating of her heart had not become obvious. 'It seems you like to punish people. Do you chastise every member of your staff in this manner?' she managed to ask in a cool voice.

His arms tightened about her again, but instead of kissing her once more he held her head firmly against his shoulder. 'How the hell I've allowed you to get under my skin I'll never know!' he gritted angrily.

Her heart leapt at his words, but she kept her tone cool. '*Under your skin?* I don't know what you mean.'

But before he could reply Barbara's voice spoke from behind them, her voice stinging with sarcasm. 'Huh, a most touching scene! Staff and boss relations appear to be growing closer every day!'

They swung round to face the girl who stood in the doorway, her face pale, her green eyes glittering with anger.

'What the devil do you want?' rasped Jonas.

She held up a letter. 'The mail came while you were out. I'm delivering this to Miss Robyn Burnett.' She turned the envelope over to read an address on the back. 'It's from somebody with the initials of S.D. who lives in James Street, Toowoomba. A boy-friend of yours, no doubt,' she jeered at Robyn. 'The poor fellow's waiting at home in Australia while you're kissing the boss in New Zealand. He probably wants to know when you'll be home. Incidentally, when *are* you leaving this place?' She sauntered into the room and tossed the letter on to the bed.

'You'll get out of this room and mind your own damned business!' Jonas snarled at her, his set jaw indicating his fury.

A low laugh escaped Barbara. 'Don't try that big boss act with me, Jonas—I've known you for too long.' She swung round to sneer at Robyn. 'I'm told this is your room now. I trust you'll be as happy as I was in it—especially when *he* comes to visit you!' And with that last thrust she tossed her head defiantly and left the room, her eyes flashing with triumph brought about by the effect her statement had had on Robyn.

Robyn heard the words with a sense of shock. She looked at Jonas, her eyes shadowed, and although she didn't know it her white face held a stricken expression.

The look he sent her was dark with anger. 'I can see that you believe her. You're quite sure she's been my mistress,' he accused. 'Okay, please yourself. Believe anything you like.'

'You're forgetting something,' she retorted coldly. 'It's not my business.'

'Isn't it? You're sure about that?'

She was too angry to seek the meaning of his question. 'How can it be my business? I've no right to be taking umbrage over the fact that you've been sneaking in here to—to visit Barbara.'

'*Sneaking*? What the hell are you talking about? I don't have to sneak about in my own home.'

'Of course—I forgot. You're the boss. Anyhow, you don't appear to be shouting denials to the high heavens. And if it's a lie it's a wonder you're not rushing after her to demand why she should say such a thing. I notice she got down those stairs fast enough after her final sally. She probably hoped you'd follow her.'

Robyn blinked to control her tears. She went to the open window, hoping that the gentle breeze stirring the curtains would help clear the turmoil from her mind, and as she took several deep breaths she realised that one fact seemed to be evident. Whatever the situation between them *had* been, it had now changed, and this at least gave her a small amount of comfort.

She waited for Jonas to leave the room so that she could let the tears fall in the comfort of privacy, but instead of hearing his footsteps cross the floor she felt his hands on her shoulders. The pressure of them sent a small shock leaping through her system, causing her to give an involuntary start.

'My touch makes you shudder?' he drawled.

'Of course not. It's just that Barbara has the power to upset me,' she admitted. At any moment she expected him to turn her round to face him. He would hold her against him to comfort her and this time she knew she would respond. But the moment did not come, and even as she waited for it his hands dropped from her shoulders and he spoke in a matter-of-fact tone.

'Well, I suppose I'd better go and check the coolstore.'

His remark recalled her to the office duties, causing her to turn to him of her own volition. 'I'll come with you to collect the wages book and the carton figures for the fruit ledger. I—I don't want to go there alone—' she admitted hesitantly.

Jonas regarded her mockingly. 'Don't tell me you're *really* afraid of her?'

She resisted the temptation to lean against him, longing to draw comfort from the shelter of his arms. 'You can call me a coward if you like, but yes, I'll admit I *am* afraid of her. I believe she'd bash my head in if given half a chance. I—I feel I don't want to go near her. I suppose it's my old habit of running away from an awkward situation instead of facing up to it. Okay, so I'm a runaway.'

The gold-flecked eyes continued to glint at her. 'I think you're overreacting to this particular situation. It's just that she's in the throes of a jealous tantrum. She's had these fits before, but she gets over them.'

'Does she, indeed? She pelted my face with plums, remember?'

His face darkened. 'I'll neither forget nor forgive her for that little trick. Mind you, it was fiery impulse because the opportunity presented itself, and what's more, I doubt that she expected the plums to find their mark.'

'You're so good at making excuses for her.' The words came bitterly. 'As for having had these fits before—how often have they occurred, and on what sort of occasions?'

He frowned and gave a slight shrug. 'There have been times when I've taken a girl out to dinner or to a cabaret,' he admitted reluctantly. 'At a later date Barbara has somehow learned of the incident and has had the temerity to seek out the girl and dress her down in no uncertain terms.'

'The poor girl—I can understand how she felt,' said Robyn. 'At the same time I'm consumed with curiosity to know what—if anything—you did about it.' She peeped at him from beneath her lashes as she uttered the last words.

'Naturally, I told Barbara what I thought of her action,' Jonas said stiffly, 'but after all, what could I do about it? I didn't hear about it until ages after it had happened. As I told you before, our fathers have been close friends since school days, and—well, Barbara's used this fact as an excuse to take a proprietorial attitude towards me. It's a state of affairs I've found better to ignore. I look upon it as something she's built up in her own mind.'

A thought struck Robyn. 'Your mothers—are they close friends?'

'Not at all. They're both, shall we say, dominant women who don't always see eye to eye.'

The picture was clear enough to Robyn. It was easy to imagine both Barbara and her mother desiring the marriage between Jonas and Barbara, but instinct seemed to tell her that Flora Ellingham did not favour this alliance. The situation struck Robyn as being amusing, causing a small chuckle to escape her.

'What's so funny?' demanded Jonas, frowning.

'I'm trying to visualise you being ruled by three domineering women.' The thought become too much and she laughed aloud.

'That'll be the day,' he retorted coldly. 'So far I've dodged the situation successfully, and I intend to go on doing so. Now, shall we go to the shed?'

As they left the room Robyn took care to lock her door. The action brought a short laugh of amusement from Jonas, but he made no comment. Minutes later, as they walked along the path towards the shed, he took her arm in a protective manner.

'Look out, she's just behind you,' he whispered mockingly.

She snatched her arm away angrily. 'It's all very well for you to joke about it! Yes, I know you're laughing at me, but I'll have to put up with it for the sake of having your company. I'll admit I'm more than grateful for it at the moment,' she assured him with sincerity.

They found the packing shed strangely silent without the workers and the rumbling noise of the grading machines. Robyn found the wages book and the day's record of cartons packed, while Jonas became engrossed in a note that had been left for him by Alf.

'Alf says the inside latch of the coolstore door's giving trouble again,' he told her. 'He says he's oiled it and that it should now open easily. I'd better have a look at it. Staff regulations state that it must be possible to open coolstore doors from the inside.'

They crossed the floor to the coolstore, where he peered at the gauge that indicated the temperature within its depths. Then he switched on the light before opening the heavy door, and they could see that the shelves emptied by Alf during the afternoon were almost covered with cartons.

Jonas said, 'Some of the girls hate coming into the coolstore. They imagine it gives them a spasm of claustrophobia. Well, it looks like another trip with more fruit to the depot tomorrow. Do you want to come with me?'

She hesitated, knowing she would love to go with him, but at the same time she realised it would be a good opportunity to make a start on the Brightlands sketch, especially as he would be absent.

'You're finding it hard to make up your mind?' he asked grimly.

His tone forced her decision. 'If you don't mind, I'll come at some other time. At present there are things I want to do at home. There's the office—and I have letters to write.'

'I see. The one you received today has to be answered at once? Somebody with the initials S.D., isn't it?' he asked sharply.

'That's right.' Robyn was puzzled by his attitude.

Had he taken Barbara's accusation seriously? Did he imagine S.D. to be one of her boy-friends? It wasn't possible that he could be *jealous*—or that he'd forgotten Sally Dawson.

'S.D. is Sally Dawson with whom I flatted in James Street,' she reminded him.

'Oh—the budding actress. Very well, please yourself if you don't want to come with me.' His tone was offhand as he tested the door latch. Nor did he make any further effort to persuade her to change her mind.

He couldn't care less, she told herself, and although she was disappointed she was not surprised. It was impossible to imagine Jonas trying to persuade anyone to do anything—yet, strangely, she had a distinct feeling that he was annoyed by her decision to remain at home. And had he *really* forgotten Sally so quickly? She doubted it. It was just part of the inscrutability that hid his thoughts from the world.

He changed the subject abruptly by indicating the wages book. 'There's a small job waiting for you between the pages,' he said. 'I want you to make a list of all the people who've worked on the place during this last year, and you'll have to add the pea harvesters who won't be in the book. It's for the end-of-year staff party. We have to give the caterers an idea of how many will be here.'

The thought of the coming party helped dispel the feeling of depression which seemed to engulf her so frequently these days. There would be dancing, Jonas had said, so surely he would dance with her, perhaps holding her closely during a slow waltz.

Later in the privacy of her room the depression descended again as she sat on the bed and read Sally's letter. 'News—news!' she had written. 'I'm engaged! Remember that fantastic theatre director who gave me such fabulous parts? At least, they were good for a second-year student—but we're not getting married until I've finished my three-year course.' The letter continued, bubbling with the effervescence of Sally's excitement as she recounted details of her future plans.

Robyn paused to rest the letter on her lap while she gazed into space. Jonas's face rose before her, and while she was glad to learn of Sally's happiness she was also acutely aware of the hopelessness of her own love for him. Would she ever really know Jonas? she wondered. She was beginning to doubt it. If only she could write by return mail and tell Sally——

Sighing wistfully, she returned to the letter, which listed the many gifts which had been showered upon Sally at various engagement parties. Then, suddenly, the letter turned to the subject of Robyn's car. 'You'll remember Joan who came to live with me when you left the flat,' Sally had written. 'She's been wondering if you'd sell it to her. She'd have it valued and you'd get a fair price for it. After all, it's only sitting in Holly's garage. I'd be pleased if you'd sell it to her as she's relying far too much on me for transport.' The last sentence brought a smile to Robyn's lips, as seldom or never had she known Sally to allow herself to be inconvenienced by anyone.

When she went downstairs for dinner Jonas was his usual urbane self. He stood up as she entered the dining room and pulled out a chair 'You look thoughtful,' he remarked.

'I've been reading Sally's letter. She's just got engaged.'

He raised one dark brow. 'Is that so? Another good man gone west. Ah well, there's nothing like an engagement to give the girls something to write about.'

'It wasn't the main point of the letter,' Robyn retorted, finding difficulty in keeping an edge from her voice. 'Sally says that the girl who's flatting with her is interested in buying my Wolseley.'

'Oh? You intend to sell it?' The hazel eyes became penetrating.

She gave a short laugh. 'Certainly not! I'll need it

when I go home. I'll fly to Brisbane and drive it down to Sydney.'

He frowned at her. 'You're so sure you'll be going home?'

'Of course. What else?' The intensity of his gaze made it difficult for her to say anything further and she could only lapse into silence. She longed to point out that while he had given her employment he had offered nothing concrete in the way of—of emotional security, and this, more than anything else, was what she craved.

Questions swirled about in her mind, three of them standing out like beacons. Loving Jonas as she did, how could she remain at Brightlands, tolerating his casual attitude towards her? Yet how could she drag herself away from the place? Despite the short time she had been there she was already attached to the old home. And, most important of all, how long would it be before she was unable to keep her love a secret from Jonas?

'You're taking a long time to answer my question,' Jonas pointed out. 'Is it so very difficult? I asked if you're so sure you'll be going home.'

'I suppose it'll depend upon Holly,' she said evasively. 'Do you realise I've seen very little of her since we arrived?'

'She's been taken over by my mother.' He sent a thoughtful glance in her direction. 'How would you cope with being taken over by Mother? Would you stand up to her—or would you run away?'

Robyn's pulses quickened slightly. What was the *real* question lurking in his mind? Pondering it carefully, she said, 'I think your mother's ideas are constructive, and I'm sure she's a woman of much experience, so she must know what's best for this place. Most of us have to learn by experience—but isn't it wiser to learn from the experience of other people?'

'Her bossiness wouldn't upset you?'

She looked at him steadily. 'That question will never arise. I'll be going home, remember?'

'Oh yes—so you said.' His eyes narrowed as he watched her.

After that a silence fell between them, although she knew he watched her with that strange enigmatic expression she was unable to fathom.

Next morning she spent some time in the office, busily listing the names in the wages book. The party wouldn't be small, she thought. Mrs Kerr knocked on the office door, politely asking for her assistance with more than one task, and it seemed to Robyn that the house-keeper was now looking upon her with more respect than when she had first arrived.

After lunch she walked about the garden, ostensibly to admire the summer blooms, but in reality to search for a suitable place from which she could sketch the house. The need for secrecy would make the project difficult, she realised, especially as she would be unable to work in her usual free manner. Instead it would be necessary to make numerous quick sketches on a small pad, and later transfer them to watercolour paper. This would have to be done in the privacy of her bedroom, where it would also be easier to check and correct the perspective of the building.

Eventually, standing hidden between rhododendron bushes, she discovered an angle view of the house that satisfied her, the composition being nicely balanced by surrounding trees and foreground of drive. It then became necessary to curb her patience until she heard the truck leave for the depot, and, as on the previous day, this did not occur until the middle of the afternoon.

It was good to have a pencil in her hand once more. As usual the complete concentration necessary for art work effectively wiped out all other thoughts from her mind. It forced her to stop thinking about Jonas, and it soothed the frustration of knowing he was so near—

and yet so far. It enabled her to control the bitter
resentment growing steadily within her—resentment fed
by the suspicion that his former caresses had been mere
cajoling tactics which would persuade her to assist
Holly across the Tasman.

Yet, despite the growing conviction of this latter
humiliating fact, she knew she would always love him,
and the desire to leave him a painting of Brightlands
done by herself became stronger than ever. At least there
might be the odd time when it could recall her to his
memory.

Secrecy for the project was not difficult, as the only
person who came near her was Tony, a boy employed
to work in the garden while Alf was busy with the fruit
pickers. He had been instructed to have the lawns cut,
the edges clipped and the garden weeded by Christmas,
and with this formidable task before him he was too
busy to waste time by peering over her shoulder.

Christmas was drawing near, and the thought of it
gave her a feeling of panic. Could she complete the
watercolour with its detailed drawing in time? There
seemed to be so much to do—the monthly accounts
were coming in to make extra office work, there were
special bonus wage packets to be made up for the staff,
and Jonas was waiting for the party guest list. Mrs Kerr
pleaded for assistance with the extra mince pies and
other foods she wanted made for the deep-freeze—yet
with it all Robyn made hasty trips outside to check on
gables or window details, or stole short periods behind
the locked door of her bedroom.

A few days before the staff party she was busily
typing a letter to order more fruit cartons when Holly
walked into the office. An exclamation of pleasure
escaped her as she left the desk to embrace the little
woman. 'Holly, how lovely to see you! Jonas's parents
are with you?'

'Yes. Robert's out at the shed and Flora's discussing
Christmas dinner with Mrs Kerr.'

Robyn looked at her critically. 'I think you've put on a little weight, Holly. You look much better than you did during the spring in Toowoomba. Are you happy? Tell me honestly.'

Holly didn't answer. Instead she avoided Robyn's direct gaze as she looked about the office, her blue eyes moving from one article to another. They rested on the rolltop desk, shifted to the cocktail cabinet and chairs beside the small table, then stared at the bookshelves. 'This could be George's office,' she whispered at last. 'Have you noticed they're almost the same?'

'Yes, I've noticed they're very similar,' Robyn admitted casually. She had caught a glimpse of tears in Holly's eyes, but decided to ignore them. Something was amiss, she feared, but Holly would tell her about it when she was ready.

The older woman sat in one of the chairs beside the table. Still avoiding Robyn's eyes, she said, 'Please go on with your work, I don't want to interrupt you. I'd just like to sit here for a while—I want to think. This office is making me see things even more clearly.'

Robyn turned back to the typewriter. She attended to another short letter and typed the envelope. Holly had something on her mind, she felt positive, and she was anxious to hear about it before Flora came into the office. 'There's something special you want to think about?' she asked at last.

'Yes. I started thinking about it soon after we arrived in New Zealand, and now this office has made up my mind for me.'

Robyn turned and faced her. 'I don't understand.' Yet vaguely at the back of her mind she did understand, but she wanted to hear the full explanation from Holly herself.

'It's really very awkward. 'I'm feeling stifled—hemmed in——'

'Oh? In what way?'

'Well—it's Flora, really,' She's determined to plan my

future, or should I say my last remaining years? She says I must sell Coolabah and buy a house near them at Westshore. But if I do that I'll find my life being ruled by Flora. My dear, I know she *means* well, but when someone tries to boss me I'm inclined to become antagonistic. I'm afraid there'd be trouble between us before very long and I'd be longing for my old home again.'

'So what has this office to do with your decision?' Robyn asked.

'Don't you see? This office, which is almost a replica of the one at Coolabah, has taken me *home*. Coolabah is the home my dear George gave me, and now I know I'll never leave it. In my heart I think I've always known. I'll stay with Flora and Robert until after New Year, and then I'll go home. Are you coming with me, or do you want to stay here?'

'I'll come with you,' Robyn found herself admitting, her eyes clouding slightly as the end of a dream appeared on the horizon.

'There'll be no need,' Holly declared firmly. 'I'll manage the journey quite easily, and then I'll find someone to live with me. I think I'm over all that attitude of not wanting to see anyone else sitting in George's chair. This trip has done me good. It's shaken a lot of silliness out of me.'

Robyn laughed, more from relief than from anything else. 'I'm so glad you're seeing it that way. I've always known that a house at Westshore could never compensate you for the loss of Coolabah and all its memories. You'd become unhappy——' She paused as Jonas interrupted from the doorway.

'What's all this about Coolabah and memories?' he asked, his eyes going from one to the other.

'Holly's decided to go home in January,' Robyn told him frankly. 'I'll be going with her.'

He strode into the room, his penetrating glare boring into Holly. 'Is this your idea, Aunt? Or is it something Robyn's persuading you to think about?'

'It's my idea entirely,' she told him calmly. 'I *am* capable of thinking of something for myself.'

'It's Mother, isn't it?' he demanded bluntly, then turned to Robyn, his eyes glinting with mockery. 'It's because of her you're returning to Australia? You're running away—*again*?'

CHAPTER NINE

THE accusation was difficult to deny. To herself Robyn freely admitted that she was running away, but how could she explain that it was not from Flora but from Jonas himself?

'Well?' he demanded in a hard voice. 'I'm waiting for an answer. Are you or are you not running away?'

Holly came to her rescue. 'What a silly thing to say, Jonas! What are you talking about? Why are you accusing Robyn of running away?' The little woman looked perplexed.

'Because that's what she's doing. She's a runaway,' he jeered.

Holly became impatient. 'What utter rubbish!' she snapped. 'Robyn hasn't run away in her life.'

'Really? How would you know, Aunt?'

'Because I know Robyn. There are times when she might find herself on the wrong track—but what does she do then? She stops, looks about her and takes a different path. That's not running away. It's known as having the good sense to change direction before the worst happens—before becoming burdened with extreme unhappiness.'

'I suppose you could look at it in that light,' Jonas conceded grudgingly. 'But in your own case, Aunt, I'd like you to be quite honest. Has Mother made you unhappy? Is she your reason for wishing to return to Australia?'

Holly was silent for a few minutes before she said, 'Very well, since you've asked for it I'll tell you the truth. You know how she loves to dominate people? She's so much stronger than I am, therefore she thinks she can rule me. Well, she can't. And I'll tell you

154

something else, Jonas—she'll dominate your poor wife—whoever she turns out to be.'

'Like hell she will,' he snarled. 'I'll make damned sure she comes near the place only when she's invited——' He broke off as Flora walked into the room, management written all over her face.

'Is somebody to be invited somewhere?' she queried, then not bothering to wait for a reply she went on, 'We're going home now, Holly. Jonas, go out and fetch your father from the shed. When he comes here he never leaves that shed. Well now,' she went on, 'I've just been telling Mrs Kerr about Christmas dinner. We'll be having it at midday and I've invited Robert's old friend Charlie Dalton and his wife and their daughter Barbara to join us here.'

'You've *what*?' Jonas exploded angrily.

'I said I've invited the Daltons to have Christmas dinner with us.'

'Did you get my permission to issue this invitation, Mother?' The question came coldly.

Flora's brows rose as she gave a short laugh. 'Your *permission*? Of course not! My dear boy, what's the matter with you? You're being quite ridiculous!'

'Am I?' His jaw was set and his temper was obviously being kept in check by an effort. 'Aren't you forgetting something, Mother?'

'What are you talking about?' Flora had drawn herself up, her manner oozing affronted dignity.

'Aren't you forgetting that this is *my* house? I say who sits at my table for Christmas dinner—or any other dinner for that matter. I know you delight in throwing your weight around, but when it comes to Brightlands I'll thank you to remember that I happen to be the boss. Is that understood?'

Flora gaped at him. 'Yes—yes, of course——'

Jonas's tone softened. 'Dear Mother, you might be able to rule Dad with an iron hand, but when it comes to this place, or anyone connected with it, those days are over for you.'

Flora subsided with a small shaky laugh. 'My dear boy, I believe you're more like me than I realised. You're right—I made a mistake. I shouldn't have asked the Daltons without first consulting you, and as it annoys you so much I'll cancel the invitation. I'll tell them—I'll find an excuse of some sort——'

Jonas frowned thoughtfully. 'No—that would upset Dad. They can come this Christmas, but it'll be the last. Mrs Kerr will also join us in the dining room, and if you think Alf's to be left out in the kitchen for Christmas dinner you're very much mistaken. It'll be quite a party.'

'A *party*—do you still have the yearly Christmas staff party?' asked Holly as though making an effort to change the subject and lighten the tense atmosphere between mother and son.

'Yes. Robyn's working on the invitation list,' Jonas told her. 'How is it going?' He turned and directed the question to Robyn.

She looked up and met his eyes. 'I think it's complete. I've been through the wages book three times,' she added as she lifted a paper from the desk and handed it to him.

He scanned the list rapidly. 'It appears to be complete. You'll find their addresses at the back of the book, and there's a box of invitation cards in one of the desk drawers.'

Flora sent critical eyes towards the desk. 'You appear to have everything under control, Robyn. That desk hasn't been so orderly since the last time I sat at it. I hope my son appreciates your efforts.' And having had the last word she swept out of the office with Holly hastening after her.

With their departure Robyn turned her attention to the desk and began searching for the invitation cards. She had no wish to meet Jonas's eyes because he would be sure to read the disappointment lurking within the depths of her own. The knowledge that Barbara and her parents would share Christmas dinner with them had come as a shock, and already she was visualising the sneering criticism and amusement in the green eyes when Jonas opened his parcel. It would make her feel like crawling under the table.

She became aware of Jonas standing behind the desk chair. The feel of his hands on her shoulders made her go rigid. She paused with one hand on a drawer, then turned her head slowly to look up at him, but found herself unable to meet his eyes.

'I thought you liked it here,' he said. 'At least, that's the impression you gave me.'

'Of course I like Brightlands. Who wouldn't?'

'Yet you're ready to leave it so soon, after New Year, in fact.'

'You—you don't understand,' she sighed.

His hands beneath her elbows forced her to a standing position, then he turned her to face him. 'Then kindly explain your reasons for hurrying away so soon. Is it that I don't pay you enough?'

Robyn stamped a foot in anger. '*Pay* me—no, of course not. If you think money is the important factor with me, then you're—you're *hopeless!*'

'Well, what is the most important factor with you?' His arms were about her and she leaned against his shoulder. His deep voice held a low enticing tone that almost betrayed her into telling the truth—into admitting that all she longed for was his love.

But how could she tell him she suspected him of being a man whose emotions were locked so deeply within himself that even he was unaware they existed? How could she find the words to suggest he dragged them to the surface and had a good look at them? Perhaps he would learn that he loved her. Or would it be Barbara?

The sigh that escaped her betrayed her dejection. Jonas looked down at her, tilted her chin and kissed her gently. Her brain shouted to her to respond, but just as her arms began to entwine his neck he released her abruptly and turned her towards the desk.

'You'd better find those cards or the day of the party will dawn before the invitations are out,' he said.

Robyn sighed again and began opening drawers. It was always the same, she thought dully. His embraces meant nothing. Like a pathetic fledgling sparrow waiting to be fed, she held up her face for kisses that were without commitment. It was a story that had no ending.

'Ah, there it is.' He extracted a cardboard box from a lower drawer and placed it on the desk before her. 'Now you'll be able to get on with the job.'

She stared at his back as he left the room, and once again the knowledge that she was nothing more than staff pounded through her brain. Then, as she worked on the list, her traitorous emotions switched to excitement as she thought of the possibility of dancing with Jonas.

The days between this incident and the staff party passed with surprising speed. Warm sunshine enabled the fruit-picking to continue without interruption, although lack of rain caused Jonas to spend time moving the irrigation pipes which threw plumes of water twirling in high wide circles over the acres of beans, sweet corn and tomatoes.

Robyn saw very little of him, but at least his absence enabled her to complete the painting of the homestead and get it into its frame. She had checked the perspective several times and had reached the stage where she could do nothing further to improve it, and she could only hope he would be passably pleased with it. In fact she was fortunate to have finished it, because more work was at hand when, the day before the party, Jonas produced a large box of decorations and told her to do what she could with them.

She decided to concentrate on the dining room, and

was on a tall ladder looping streamers across the window pelmet when strong fingers clasped her legs and slid between her ankles and knees.

Jonas's deep voice spoke from below her. 'You've got the loveliest legs, Robyn—but I told you that in Toowoomba——'

The ladder shook. 'Stop it—*stop it at once*—do you want me to fall?' Shocks went through her as his hands pulled her down and encircled her waist. 'What are you trying to do?'

'I'm trying to get you off the ladder. I've got something to show you—something I think you'll like.' He led her through the kitchen to where the truck was parked in the yard near the back door. On the tray was a young fir tree set in a large tub.

'A Christmas tree!' she exclaimed, delighted. 'It's lovely—but I thought you intended using a small pine from near the river.'

'I changed my mind when I saw firs for sale at a nursery. Later it can be planted. It's much better than chopping a tree.'

Alf arrived with Tony, the boy from the garden, and between the three of them the fir in its tub was carried into the dining room, where it was set near the fireplace and within reach of a power plug. Its branches towered above the mantelpiece, its short stiff needle-covered boughs jutting out as though pleading for decorations.

Jonas found a can of artificial snow and within moments the branches had been sprayed to glistening whiteness. Then he delved into the box of decorations and brought out two sets of small coloured lights which he arranged on the tree. When the power was switched on the tree glowed with the magic of fairyland, but Robyn was not satisfied until she had added shining glass baubles and glittery tinsel streamers. As she placed them with care she became aware of Jonas standing close beside her, and of Alf observing them from the doorway.

'That's really a sight to be seen,' Alf remarked.

'You think the tree looks okay?' Jonas asked casually.

'It sure does—but I wasn't meaning the tree, even if it *is* the best we've had since I've been here.'

'Oh? Then explain yourself,' drawled Jonas.

'I mean it's a mighty fine sight to see you and Robyn working on the tree together. Go to it, lassie,' added Alf with a chuckle as he disappeared into the hall.

Robyn flushed as she glanced at Jonas. 'What does he mean?' she asked, feeling she had to say something.

'I wouldn't have a clue,' he replied, his face expressionless.

The day of the party was cloudless and warm. Jonas closed the shed at mid-afternoon, and there was an air of suppressed excitement as the pickers and packers went home early, but by six o'clock they had returned, accompanied by husbands and boy-friends.

By that time the carpet in the wide hall had been rolled back and the floor was ready for dancing. The stereo record player and its speakers had been placed in their positions, and electricians had strung coloured lights overhead. Two men from a Hastings liquor store had set up a bar to serve drinks, and the caterers van had arrived with a quantity of food.

Robyn was feeling distinctly nervous. She had had little to do with the packing shed staff, and tonight she would be mingling with them on a closer basis. She knew that they would be watching her closely, comparing her with Barbara, and no doubt criticising her. During the day she had been busy arranging flowers and placing them about the house, thankful to have learnt a little of the art from her mother, whose floral arrangements were always a feature of her boutiques. She had almost finished when Jonas walked in. He stood still, staring at the vases without comment, then went upstairs to shower and change.

Later, after her own shower, Robyn applied fresh

make-up with special care, then reached for her apricot dress with its soft feminine lines. During the spring in Toowoomba it had been a gift from her mother, who had written, 'This has just come in. I think it's so absolutely *you* that I'm sending it at once. Hope you can find a special occasion and that it'll be your lucky, good-time dress.' It had been her mother's way of saying 'for heaven's sake stop sitting round in that flat—go out and enjoy yourself.' But the special occasion never seemed to arise.

She put the dress on and surveyed her reflection in the long mirror. Mother had been right—as usual. The dress was flattering and seemed to do things for her. She knew she looked nice, and her spirits rose.

When she went downstairs she discovered that Holly had arrived with Flora and Robert Ellingham. Flora swept an approving glance over her dress. 'My dear, you look really lovely,' she commented. 'And the flowers look as if they've been arranged by a professional florist.'

It was as good as praise from royalty, and Robyn's spirits soared even higher.

'She's right,' whispered Holly. 'Tonight you look quite beautiful. Tell me, has Jonas said anything about—well, you know what I mean——?'

Robyn gave a small hollow laugh. She knew only too well what Holly meant. 'No. Nor does he have any intentions in that direction, so you can forget it, Holly. Do you still intend to fly home in January?'

'Yes—but I haven't dared mention it to Flora, There's plenty of time for *that* particular argument. Are you still coming with me?'

Before Robyn could answer Barbara walked into the room, arriving just late enough to make an impressive entrance. Her red hair was arranged in a sophisticated style and her vivid green dress made her eyes look like emeralds. 'Hi, everyone—I'm here!' she called gaily. 'Where's Jonas?'

Robyn looked at Holly. 'I think you can rely on the fact that I'll be on the plane with you,' she said quietly. Her spirits had already begun to slide downwards.

Holly sensed her dejection. 'Snap out of it, Robyn,' she said sharply. 'You'll get nowhere by allowing that girl's vivacity to swamp you with gloom. Now come and introduce me to some of the staff, otherwise I'll be standing round like a ninny.'

It was something to do, and Robyn was grateful for the task. She could see Flora being pleasant to people, and almost unconsciously she followed her example until, before she realised it, she was laughing and at ease.

It was automatic for Flora to take over the role of hostess. She moved graciously among the guests, making sure to chat amicably with each one, while Jonas and the two barmen attended to any empty glasses. Savouries were handed round until the caterers, who had taken over the kitchen, began to arrange forks, plates and numerous containers of food on the dining room table.

Robyn was amazed at the extent of the menu. When Jonas had mentioned a party she had imagined the staff coming in for a few drinks and coffee—but this was a function which indicated that he really appreciated their work in the orchard and shed. And while they were free to examine the interior of the old home their main activities were confined to the lounge, dining room, and the hall where the stereo invited dancing in the mystic atmosphere of coloured lights.

Robyn noticed that Jonas had already danced with several of the girls and realised he was being the perfect host. She waited patiently for her turn to come, but he made no attempt to approach her. Eventually, the first person who asked her to dance was young Tony, and, frustrated, she went to the hall with him.

Other people were forming partners on the floor, and from the corner of her eye she could see Jonas and

Barbara, who seemed to be dancing rather closely. At times a veiled glance slid in her direction, and it needed little intuition to know that Barbara was talking about her, although Jonas, staring over the red head, wore his mask-like expression. The thought of Barbara discussing her was irritating, but she shrugged it away as being of no consequence and threw herself into dancing with Tony.

The long-playing record seemed to go on for ever, but eventually the music stopped. Tony escorted her back to the settee in the lounge and settled down beside her, apparently with the intention of remaining there for the rest of the evening, but, mercifully, a girl nearer his own age claimed his attention.

The music began again and couples drifted back to the hall. Robyn's eyes searched the room for Jonas, longing for him to ask her to dance, but he was again engrossed with members of the staff. Face the truth, she told herself crossly, he has no intention of dancing with you. If it hadn't been for young Tony you'd have been a real wallflower——

And then Alf's voice spoke in her ear. 'Would you take a turn with an old man?' he asked.

She forced a gay smile. 'Of course, Alf—I thought you'd never ask!' Which was not quite the truth.

They had made barely one turn of the hall when she saw Barbara drag Jonas through the door and on to the floor. She watched as they danced and knew that the girl's arms were entwined about his neck as she gazed up into his face. The sight enraged her, but she fought for control and chatted to Alf.

He sent a glance across the floor. 'Do you think they make a handsome couple?' he asked teasingly.

'No, I don't,' she snapped, irritated by the question.

'Has he asked you to dance yet?'

Robyn shook her head, too miserable to answer.

Suddenly the music changed as a loud band hammered out a primitive beat on drums and electric guitars. It stirred the couples who danced beneath the diffused glow of red, yellow, blue and green lights into a writhing, twisting group who bobbed up and down as each one did his or her own thing to the sound of the raucous music.

Robyn found herself swaying to the rhythm as she faced Alf on the edge of the crowd, and as she turned she could see Jonas, his expression seeming to be grimly amused by the exaggerated contortions displayed by Barbara, who twirled and gyrated with abandon. When would Jonas dance with her? Robyn wondered wistfully.

Somehow their dancing took them nearer the stereo and she became aware of the band's drums throbbing loudly in her ears. For a short time she closed her eyes as she danced, then, when she opened them, it was Jonas instead of Alf who moved in rhythm beside her. She had no idea how or when the change had been made, but there he was, watching her with that cynical and enigmatic expression she was learning to recognise, while Alf danced with Barbara.

The beating of the drums became even more difficult to bear, hurting her ears and causing her to move away from their deafening clamour. Jonas followed her, anger flashing from the hazel eyes.

'You don't want to dance with me?' he shouted in her ear.

'It's not that—it's the music—it's so loud,' she tried to explain. 'It's ghastly—I can't bear it!'

'Okay, let's move away.' His hand on her arm guided her to the other end of the hall. As he did so the tempo of the music changed to a beat of three and his arms went about her, holding her closely as they danced to the strains of a waltz. Robyn was bemused by the magnetic sensation of his body moving against her own, but told herself it was the kaleidoscope of colour swaying overhead and the continued throbbing in her ears that obliterated all sense of proportion from her mind. That was why she clung to him as they danced—at least, it was what she tried to believe.

Somebody turned the volume of the stereo down to a lower pitch and the music now whispered the melody of yet another slow and seductive waltz. The soft tones beat a dreamy rhythm into Robyn's brain, and as Jonas's arms gripped her until they almost merged as one person she became aware of muscled thighs, a broad chest and the pressure of his chin resting against the softness of her hair. Her former resentment towards him melted as she gave herself up to the rapture of drifting in his arms. Their gliding steps matched with perfect unity, and as she closed her eyes she could have been floating away on a cloud.

When the music stopped he released her so abruptly she found herself swaying and was forced to lean against him for support. He peered at her anxiously. 'You're all right? You look very pale. Your eyes are like burnt holes in a blanket.'

She laughed shakily. 'Thank you—you're so flattering!'

'I suppose you'll think I'm flattering you if I say you look really beautiful tonight—in fact I've never seen you look so lovely.' His deep voice held a ring of sincerity.

Unable to believe her ears, she said, 'Thank you again. I'll admit I'm beginning to feel a bit jaded.'

'You must be tired. I know you've had a big day. And you needn't think I haven't noticed those charming floral arrangements you've arranged about the room.'

His words of praise sent a glow through her veins and brought colour to her cheeks. 'Fresh air is what I really need,' she explained. 'The rooms have become stuffy with so much cigarette smoke, it's beginning to affect my eyes by making them sting. If you'll excuse me I think I'll go outside for a while.'

'A good idea,' he agreed. 'I could do with a breath of fresh air myself.' He took her arm and led her towards the front door.

'I don't want to keep you from your guests,' she protested. 'I'll be quite all right.'

'So will the guests,' he assured her. 'We'll examine the roses by moonlight. It's the best time to examine roses——'

'I'm afraid I picked them all this morning.' Her heart was hammering as he took her arm while descending the front steps, and when he continued to keep her close to his side as they crossed the lawn to the main rosebed she felt positively breathless.

'Here's one you missed,' said Jonas as they reached the edge of the extensive oval bed. He snapped off an opening bloom and, turning her to face him, tucked it in the cleavage at the low-cut neckline of her dress. 'I happen to know the name of this particular rose,' he went on softly. 'It's known as First Love. It's a delicate pink with a long bud.'

Hope stirred within her breast, but the next moment she reminded herself that she was being stupid. Nevertheless she looked up at him wonderingly. Was there a subtle meaning hidden within the words? But the moonlight cast shadows over his brow and there was no way of reading the expression in his eyes. Hope leapt again as his fingers beneath her chin tilted her face upwards. Tingles invaded her body as his lips rested on her own, exploring and waiting for her to respond, but suddenly she was filled with a disturbing conviction that made her stiffen and draw back.

'You're being nice to me again,' she accused quietly. 'You want me to do something for you. What is it? I know—it's Holly. You want me to persuade her to remain in New Zealand. Is that it?'

Jonas laughed lightly. 'What a suspicious little person you are! No, of course it's not Holly.'

'But you do want me to do something for you? I can sense it.'

His voice became cool. 'Are you suggesting that the only time I'm at all pleasant to you is when I want something?'

'It does seem to work out that way,' she told him frankly. 'I've noticed it on more than one occasion. What is it this time?'

'Nothing,' he gritted harshly. 'Forget it.'

But she was now curious. 'Please tell me—I *know* you want me to do something for you.'

'Okay, I'll admit I'd like your assistance. I want you to play a few Christmas carols on the piano. We always end the staff party with a sing-song, although Mother usually plays—reluctant as she is to do so.'

The request surprised Robyn. 'Is that all? It's not much to ask. You want only carols?'

'No. I'd like a few popular songs before the carols. Then, when I give you the nod, I want *Auld Lang Syne*.'

'You mean you want the party brought to an end? Nothing finishes things like the singing of *Auld Lang Syne*.'

'That's right. Have you looked at the time? It's well after midnight. I don't want a lot of dead-beats here in the morning. I don't want people falling off ladders or selecting blemished fruit because they're too tired to keep their eyes open. So—will you do it for me?'

Robyn longed to say she'd do anything for him. Instead she said, 'Have you forgotten that Barbara warned me against *thumping* on the piano? She said your mother objects to it being touched, remember?'

'Take no notice of what Barbara says,' Jonas growled tersely.

'Very well.' She gave a small laugh. 'You know, you could have asked me without going to all this trouble of bringing me out into the moonlight and so forth. I mean—you've been almost romantic!'

'And you don't like it?'

'To be honest, I've loved it,' she told him.

'Well, at least that's something. In the meantime I'd like to assure you I had no idea that the only time I appear to be amiable is when I want something.' Jonas sounded decidedly huffy. 'And as you're so sure I can't do a thing without an atom of sincerity behind it we'd better go inside.'

They crossed the lawn in silence. When they reached the lounge they found Flora in conversation with Barbara and her mother. Robyn hesitated before interrupting their discussion, then, gripping courage firmly, she approached the trio.

She put a hand on Flora's arm. 'Excuse me, Mrs Ellingham—Jonas has asked me to play a few songs and carols. Is that all right with you? I mean, you won't mind if I play your piano?'

Flora beamed. '*Mind?* Of course not. That poor neglected piano isn't played enough. Play it as often as you like, my dear. Who on earth could have made you think otherwise?'

'Thank you.' Robyn glanced at Barbara, but the vivacious redhead avoided her eyes. Then she made her way to the piano, where she followed Jonas's instructions by playing several well-known songs. For a while little notice was taken of her efforts, but within a short time the guests began to gather round the piano, and as her fingers rippled over the keys their voices rose in chorus after chorus.

Jonas, she noticed, had a pleasant baritone, and Barbara's voice was passable as she took his arm, gazed up into his face and tried to make it appear as though they were the main singers. Her unnesessary closeness to Jonas almost amounted to possessiveness, and, glancing at them across the strings revealed by the large open lid, Robyn became so irritated she switched from love songs to carols. Eventually she caught Jonas's eye. He gave her a brief nod and she knew it was time for *Auld Lang Syne*.

As the familiar Scottish air rolled from the Steinway the staff formed a large circle to join hands and sing the words written so long ago by Robert Burns. How universal the old song is, Robyn thought. It closes social functions in most English-speaking countries——

But suddenly her thoughts were broken into as a cry of rage came from the circle of guests. Barbara snatched her hands from the two people on either side of her and marched towards the piano.

'Don't you *dare* play that!' she shrieked at Robyn. 'You're deliberately breaking up the party,' she accused in fury. 'Jonas, tell her to stop it at once!'

However, as she went towards the piano she was waylaid by Jonas before she could try to slam the lid shut. Robyn completed *Auld Lang Syne* as though nothing had happened, and as the guests crossed their arms and the circle drew in, Barbara's outburst was ignored.

CHAPTER TEN

As a special concession, work began an hour later next day. Men arrived to remove the coloured lights from the hall, the carpet was relaid on the floor, and between them Robyn and Mrs Kerr soon had the house in order.

Jonas made no comment concerning Barbara's behaviour towards Robyn during the singing of *Auld Lang Syne*. It was almost as though he condoned it, she thought bitterly as she decided that she too would ignore the episode. She was glad she hadn't been intimidated into leaving the piano, and thankful that the volume of the combined voices had been sufficient to drown the wrong notes she was playing as her fingers stumbled over the keys.

Mrs Kerr, however, was not so ready to allow Barbara's rudeness to pass unnoticed, and she was not satisfied until she had apologised to Robyn and had had her say on the matter. 'I'm sorry about what happened,' she admitted. 'I always say it's that red hair of hers. The poor girl can't help herself. She makes up her mind about having something and she's not satisfied until she's got it. Nor does she care *how* she gets it. And let me tell you that most of her actions are done on the spur of the moment.'

'There's no need to tell me about her impulsive actions, Mrs Kerr,' Robyn reminded her. 'If you don't mind, I'd rather not talk about Barbara.'

'Ah well, perhaps I don't blame you. But Christmas will be here so soon and that'll be a happy time, I'm sure.' Mrs Kerr brightened visibly at the thought of the festive season.

Robyn gave a short laugh. 'A happy time? With Barbara here? I'll probably spend the day in my room!'

170

Mrs Kerr was shocked. 'My dear, you can't do that! The Ellinghams and Mrs Hollingford will be here. They'd be most upset if you remained in your room.'

'Yes, I suppose you're right.' Nevertheless Robyn was unable to rid herself of a feeling of foreboding every time she thought of Christmas Day.

The weather continued to be fine and warm until Christmas Eve, when a sudden change to southerly winds brought a drop in the temperature. Dark clouds billowed over the distant ranges, and despite the previous blue skies Christmas Day was wet and cool.

Jonas lit a fire in the dining room. The leaping flames gave the room a cheerful atmosphere and threw a pink glow on to the artificial snow glistening on the branches of the tree. He dropped several pine logs on the hearth before turning to Robyn, who was adjusting several baubles which had fallen from the tree during the party.

'I'm afraid you'll find the New Zealand weather quite unpredictable,' he warned, frowning towards the window.

She sent him a level glance. 'The weather's not the only unpredictable commodity to be found round these parts.'

'Oh?' He turned questioning eyes upon her. 'What do you mean by that remark?'

'One never knows where one stands—with some people.'

'Kindly explain yourself.' His voice was sharp.

But she had no wish to explain herself, and was thankful when his parents and Holly walked into the room. They all bore gift-wrapped parcels which were placed round the base of the tree. 'Thank heaven for a fire!' Flora exclaimed. 'Compliments of the season, Robyn dear, I hope you'll have a happy Christmas Day with us.' Then, to Robyn's surprise, Flora placed affectionate arms about her and kissed her warmly. It lifted her spirits a little and made her feel more like one of the family.

The extra parcels round the tree made it easier for Robyn to put her own parcels beneath the branches without the large one for Jonas looking too conspicuous. She carried it downstairs when he was outside with his father and when everyone else seemed to be occupied— but even then it was necessary to change the positions of other parcels so that it was pushed into the background.

It was almost midday when the Daltons arrived for Christmas dinner, which was scheduled for one o'clock. Barbara wore a smart turquoise suit that really did things for her and made her eyes look more blue than green. It also made Robyn feel insignificant in her yellow and white outfit which she had considered would be warm enough despite the coolness of the day.

The party gathered in the lounge where Flora, Holly and Mrs Dalton settled themselves in a corner to chat. And while Robert, Alf and Mr Dalton discussed topics of mutual interest Jonas attended to the drinks. The two girls were therefore thrown together, and contrary to Robyn's expectations, Barbara was surprisingly pleasant to her. From the numerous questions she asked about Toowoomba and the Darling Downs Institute one would have imagined her to be genuinely interested, but deep within her mind Robyn suspected that Barbara was merely putting on an act of friendship.

Jonas approached them, a crystal sherry decanter in his hand. As he refilled their glasses he said with mock severity, 'I'm glad to see you two girls getting on so well. It must be the sherry.'

Barbara laughed gaily. 'Dear Jonas, *of course* we're the *best* of friends.' Then, changing the subject abruptly and despite Robyn's presence, she said, 'I haven't put your present on the tree. It's here. Open it and put it on.' She pressed a small square gift-wrapped parcel into his hand.

He looked at it doubtfully. 'Put it on? What is it? A tiepin, or cufflinks——?'

She laughed again. 'Neither. Open it and see—and then slip it on.' She gazed expectantly into his face.

Watching Jonas with interest, Robyn noticed that his eyes narrowed thoughtfully as he removed the Christmas wrapping from the small parcel. 'It's a signet ring,' he remarked coolly. 'You know perfectly well that I never wear rings.'

'But you'll wear this one for me,' Barbara declared with confidence as she threw her head back seductively while gazing at him through half-closed lids.

'We'll discuss it later,' was all he said. Then, slipping the ring and its box into his jacket pocket, he moved away to refill Holly's glass.

Barbara sighed as he left them. 'Isn't he the most frustrating man? I suppose he doesn't want to wear it before he's put the ring on *my* finger. You probably know we're almost engaged.'

'No, I didn't know,' Robyn said gravely. Was this a fact—or was it merely wishful thinking on Barbara's part? she wondered.

The meal passed pleasantly with quips and jokes flying across the table. Alf made them laugh with humorous stories, but for Robyn the Christmas dinner had been ruined by the thought of Jonas wearing a ring given to him by Barbara. *Would* he relent and wear it? If so, she was thankful she wouldn't be here for long to see its gold glinting on his finger.

The gift-opening session began at the end of the meal while they were still sitting at the table. Glasses of champagne were beside them as Jonas handed the parcels around, and as each one was opened exclamations of genuine pleasure echoed about the room.

Robyn and Barbara each received identical bottles of expensive perfume from Jonas, a fact which told Robyn quite clearly that he thought no more of her than he did of Barbara. The knowledge cut into her as sharply as the wound from a knife, but she knew there was nothing she could do about it, so she sat in silent misery while the surrounding happy chatter passed over her head.

After what seemed to be an age the painting was dragged from behind the tree. It was the last of the gifts to be brought forward, and by that time Robyn's state had changed to one of jittery nervous tension. Had she taken sufficient care with the perspective? Was the sketch of the house correct in every detail? But more important—*would he like it?* She gave a resigned sigh. Oh well, she couldn't help it if he didn't. She'd done her best.

She watched while Jonas read the card on the parcel. She knew he was feeling its weight and was not surprised when he said, 'This has a familiar feel about it. I can't help wondering if it's something I carried along the street in Hastings.'

She did not reply but waited patiently for him to untie the bright red ribbon. At the same time she realised that Jonas was not the only person to be intrigued by its contents, as a sudden hush had fallen on the room while everyone watched and waited for the gift wrapping to be torn aside. At last, with the painting revealed, there were exclamations of surprise and admiration for Robyn's skill, although Jonas continued to stare at it without speaking.

Robyn's heart sank. 'You don't like it?' she asked timidly.

'*Like it?* I can't tell you how much I like it. I'm delighted with it.' His voice had become husky. He crossed the room to where she sat at the table, and taking her hands he pulled her to her feet. His arms went about her as he held her closely in a warm embrace. Nor did he seem to care about the presence of the others as his lips found hers in an emotional kiss that showed more than gratitude for the gift. Robyn's heart pounded as she clung to him and responded with unashamed ardour.

'Bravo!' said Alf. 'And about time too!'

Alf's words seemed to break the spell, but as Jonas released her he continued to gaze down into her upturned face. Flushed, she turned to regain her seat at the table, but was suddenly appalled by the expression she caught on Barbara's face. The redhaired girl had gone pale and her green eyes glittered with venom as they sent flashes of naked hatred in her direction. However, it was only momentary, and the next instant Barbara was admiring the painting, although her voice lacked sincerity.

But Robyn had also caught the questioning glances that had flashed between Flora and Robert Ellingham, and between Flora and Holly. Had Jonas found love at last? the veiled looks seemed to ask. She longed to tell them they had no need to worry—that he had no real love for her and that soon she would have flown home across the Tasman.

The thought of doing so deepened her depression until a prickling round her eyes warned that she was in danger of shedding tears. The thought of having to explain them would be mortifying, so she left the room and hurried upstairs, where she renewed her make-up. A glance at the window showed that the heavy rain had stopped, and, feeling in need of fresh air, she went outside to stand on the balcony. She was still gazing at the rain-drenched garden when Jonas came to stand beside her.

'Are you all right, Robyn?' he asked. 'I saw you leave the room and wondered if you were upset—about something.'

She turned away from him. 'Upset about something? Like what?'

'Like being kissed in front of the others. It didn't embarrass you too much?'

'Not really. I think they realised you were pleased with the painting and that you were just saying thank you. They probably guessed the kiss didn't mean a thing—in any other way.'

'And you—what did you feel about it?'

'Oh, I knew it was your usual kiss and run type of thing,' she shrugged. 'You've kissed me several times now, Jonas. Not one of them mean anything, so what else would you expect me to feel about it?'

'I notice you didn't kiss me for the bottle of perfume I gave you—not even a tiny wee peck.'

Barbara spoke from the doorway behind them. '*I'll* kiss you for the perfume you gave *me*, Jonas. Thank you so much—it's my favourite and I love it.' She stepped out on to the balcony and flung her arms round his neck.

Robyn found herself unable to watch Barbara's performance, the sight of the long fingers running through Jonas's dark hair infuriating her to the extent of forcing her to leave the balcony. She ran downstairs and joined the others who were sitting round the fire that had been lit in the lounge.

Jonas and Barbara came down a few minutes later. Jonas was frowning, and Robyn thought she detected a grim line about his mouth. She noticed that Barbara was a little paler than usual, and knew instinctively that Jonas had been harsh to her. An unexpected sympathy for the girl rose within her.

The remainder of the afternoon passed pleasantly enough. Heavy rain fell to make the atmosphere even cooler than it had been and more logs were thrown on the fire. The men discussed topics ranging from cricket to politics while the women found subjects of interest to themselves. It was not difficult to see that Barbara was bored. Robyn noticed she watched the windows for the rain to stop, and the moment this happened she reminded her parents that guests might call in and that it was time they went home.

As they stood up to take their leave Flora said to Barbara, 'Go to the shed and get two or three cartons of peaches for your mother. Robyn dear, go with her and help her carry them.'

To go to the shed with Barbara was almost the last thing Robyn wanted to do, but she could think of no good reason for refusing. She was also surprised at Barbara's affability as they dodged the puddles while walking along the path, and by the time they were inside the shed she was almost wondering if the flash of hatred she thought she had seen when Jonas had kissed her had been her imagination. Barbara could be so nice and such good fun when it suited her. It was easy to see why the pickers and packers liked her, Robyn realised.

They peered into a bin of peaches waiting to be graded when work began again, and although Robyn thought they looked delicious, they failed to satisfy Barbara. 'Not those ones,' she said. 'They're only second grade. When Mrs Ellingham gives anything away it's always *first* grade. She said to fetch *cartons*, which are the first grade, and they're all in the coolstore.' She moved towards the end of the shed.

Robyn's gaze lingered on the bin of peaches which, to her eyes, seemed to be unblemished. She wondered if Jonas knew his mother was blithely giving away cartons ready for export when this good fruit would have done just as well. However, there was nothing she could do about it.

She crossed the shed and stood watching while Barbara, having switched on the coolstore light, struggled with the difficult latch of the heavy door. At first it seemed as though it was refusing to move, but at last it swung open, causing a rush of chilly air to surround them.

Barbara said, 'You hold this door while I get a couple of cartons.' She went into the coolstore and moments later emerged with two of the smaller sized cardboard boxes. 'Now you go and get one,' she commanded.

'But you've already got two,' protested Robyn.

'Mrs Ellingham said two or three, remember? Hurry

up—I don't want to swing this door right back—it's so heavy.'

As Robyn stepped into the coolstore she was conscious of a feeling of cold premonition. She told herself not to be a fool, but even as she raised her hands to take a carton from the shelf she heard the door close behind her. She swung round to stare at its blank wall and the next moment she was in darkness. Barbara had shut her in and had switched off the light.

The shock of it left her gasping, and she uttered a terrified shriek which seemed to echo round the walls and shelves before it bounced back at her. *'Barbara— Barbara!'* she screamed. 'Open the door—*please, Barbara, open the door!'*

In an effort to gain control of herself she took several deep breaths before shouting, 'Okay Barbara, you've had your little joke by scaring me stiff—now open the door, *please!* I'm well aware that you hate me, but I also know you wouldn't leave me in here to freeze——' But no answer came to break the dark silence surrounding her.

And then she remembered there was an inner latch to the door. Hadn't Alf said it was giving trouble and that he'd oiled it? No doubt Barbara expected her to discover it and let herself out. Trembling, she felt her way along the shelves until her fingers encountered the smooth cold flatness of the door, and then the latch was easy enough to find. But despite her desperate struggles she was unable to move it, and at last she had to accept that the latch was stuck fast and that it was beyond her to make it budge. 'So much for your oil, Alf!' she panted aloud, her voice again echoing in her ears as she began a fruitless hammering on the door.

Claustrophobia began to crowd in upon her. The darkness bore down upon her like a crushing depression, the utter blackness seeping into her head until she imagined it was piercing her brain. It went in through her eyes, taking possession of her mind until rising panic forced her to renew her hammering on the door with frenzied desperation.

Panic grew steadily until it had her in a firm grip. Screams began to leave her, but they brought nothing except a tightening in her throat and a constriction in her chest that made breathing almost impossible. Her heart thumped with terror until at last, exhausted and gasping, she slumped against the door before sliding to the floor where she remained crouched in a pathetic heap.

As time passed the first wave of panic began to subside and her numbed senses warned she must not allow it to rise again and take control. She must think with clarity and decide what to do for the best. But what could she do other than wait? Surely Barbara would open the door soon. *Or would she?* If Barbara expected her to find the latch and get out by her own efforts it was unlikely she would return to open the door, and in that case it would be necessary to stay there for hours and hours, because there was no other way out.

She got to her feet and struggled with the latch again, but it was immovable, and it was then that she began to feel the cold. The chill of the coolstore was getting to her, penetrating the medium-weight yellow and white suit and her underwear. It was causing gooseflesh all over her body, and it was making her shiver as though gripped by an ague until she crouched, hugging herself.

How much cold could her system tolerate? she wondered. The coolstore was refrigerator temperature rather than deep freeze, but could she stand it for the entire night—all tomorrow—and the next night? The staff were given Christmas Day and Boxing Day as holidays, which meant she would have to endure the cold until they came back to work, unless someone came looking for her. No doubt there would be a search along the riverbank—but who would think of looking in the coolstore? What was the term given when the body temperature sank below the usual level? Hypothermia? She had heard of elderly people dying from its results.

She sprang to her feet from the crouching position and began jumping up and down, flinging her arms about her in an effort to keep her circulation moving. And then she recalled having heard that hypothermia was a state where the energy should be conserved. She shouldn't be jumping up and down. In any case she couldn't feel her feet, because they were numb. Her thin sandals had given her no protection at all from the cold concrete floor.

As the minutes dragged by she made several more futile attempts to move the door latch, until at last, sobbing with fear and exhaustion, she collapsed on the floor once more. She had no idea how long she had been there, huddled and weeping and gripped by violent shaking, but suddenly it seemed as though something was happening to her mind. The place seemed to be flooded with light and she thought she was floating. It was almost as though someone had lifted her from the floor, while through the depths of her misery she even imagined she heard the blessed sound of Jonas's voice.

'Robyn, my darling, what the hell are you doing here——?'

She was unable to control her sobs and could do no more than shake her head in a vague way. Yet somehow she knew Jonas was there, that he had really picked her up and she was being carried to some place. Darling—had Jonas actually said—*darling*? She felt herself being laid on a soft surface and knew he had blankets wrapped about her while he rubbed her body, her arms and legs, and that he had paused only to plug in an electric jug.

He removed her sandals to massage her feet, his busy hands working on her circulation while the blankets added their warmth. 'Speak to me, Robyn,' he pleaded. 'Speak to me, my darling!'

Darling. There it was again. She hadn't been dreaming when she'd heard it the first time. 'Where am I?' she asked, her teeth chattering.

'In Alf's bedroom at the end of the shed. His bed was the nearest place for warmth. Your body has to be reheated gradually, otherwise I'd have turned on his heater and electric blanket. I don't think your blood temp has dropped too low, but we're not taking any risks. See if you can sip this sweet tea. Alf always uses teabags. Little does he know there's a girl in his bed!'

Robyn giggled and the cup clattered against her teeth while the painful tension began to leave her body. Jonas allowed her only a small amount of the hot liquid before taking the cup away from her, then he lay beside her on the bed, his arms holding her closely against his body as he rubbed her back with a firm but gentle movement.

'Now then, tell me how you became locked in the coolstore?' he demanded.

Robyn was silent, knowing there was no reason why she should lie to protect Barbara from Jonas's wrath, yet hesitating to tell him the facts. A miserable telltale, he'd think her to be.

'It was Barbara, wasn't it?' he pursued. 'You may as well admit it. I can see her trademark quite clearly.'

'Well, yes, it was Barbara, but she probably thought I'd find the inside latch and get out without any trouble. I found the latch all right, but I couldn't move it.' It was impossible to prevent her own arms from creeping round his waist as she snuggled against him. 'How—how did you find me?' she managed to ask.

'That particular project took far too long,' he growled. 'After the Daltons had left I searched through the house, but you weren't to be found, nor had anybody seen you——'

'*You* were searching for *me*?' She could hardly believe it. 'Why?'

'Because there's something I'm anxious to learn,' he

told her patiently. 'It's something that only you can tell me.'

'Oh? I suppose it's something to do with the painting—and in that case it's something that can be discussed later. But now I want to know how you found me,' she pleaded.

'It was really Mother who gave me the clue. When I asked her where you were she admitted she'd sent you with Barbara to fetch peaches from the shed. When Barbara returned to the house without you she told Mother you'd decided to take a walk along the riverbank while the rain had stopped because you felt the need for fresh air. Mother then remarked to me that she hoped you wouldn't ruin those pretty sandals on the riverbank—and suddenly I knew you hadn't gone there at all. I knew Barbara had lied. I also realised that the peaches I'd seen being shoved into the back of the Daltons' car were from the coolstore instead of the bin. Well, the fact that two girls had been to the coolstore and only one had returned made me wonder if Barbara had been up to one of her tricks, so I came racing to the shed.'

'Thank heavens you did! Thank you for finding me.' Robyn sighed contentedly, savouring these precious moments in his arms, until she recalled his earlier words. 'You said you were searching for me because there was something you wanted to know. What was it?'

'Only if—you'll marry me.'

The words took her breath away. She moved her position so that she could look into his face. 'I think the cold must have affected my brain! I almost imagine that you—that you——'

'That I proposed to you? You're right, I did. Will you marry me, Robyn? I love you so very much.'

She nodded, finding herself unable to speak. Instead she lifted her face for the kisses she hungered for, and as their lips met her heart hammered from such sheer joy it sent a flood of extra warmth flowing through her body.

'You're feeling better?' murmured Jonas as his lips nuzzled against her neck. 'You're feeling rational and in your right senses?'

'Yes, I'm feeling quite normal, if one can be normal on a cloud.'

'Then tell me you love me. Say you'll marry me soon.'

'Oh yes—! Darling Jonas, I love you. Yes, yes—of course I'll marry you whenever you like——'

'You'll be happy to live at Brightlands? You've seen what life can be like—so busy for much of the year.'

'Of course I'll be happy at Brightlands. The thought of leaving was becoming unbearable. I just want to be with you, Jonas.'

'Darling, when did you first realise you love me?' he murmured as his lips brushed her closed lids.

'I knew in Toowoomba,' she admitted shyly. 'And you——?'

'I also knew in Toowoomba,' he said, 'but that was only part of it. I had to make sure you'd be happy at Brightlands, which was so far away and so very different from the life you'd known in Australia. It was most important to get you here to see the place and to watch your reaction to it. I couldn't finish what I'd begun in Toowoomba until I knew the answers to those questions, which could be found only at Brightlands.'

'Is that what you meant when you said there was something to be completed at a later date?' asked Robyn. 'I've remembered those words quite often, but found them difficult to understand.'

'You understand them now?'

'Yes, I think so—although I don't mind telling you it was a shock to find you so cool when I arrived in New Zealand.'

'That was because I had to keep myself under control and my feet on the ground. There have been many times when I've longed to sweep you into my arms and just hold you there, but I had to wait to see how you'd contend with Mother. She might have frightened you away. Do you think you'll be able to cope with her domineering spirit, my darling? I'll be beside you——'

Robyn laughed. 'I'll cope. Nor will I run away from her. I don't find her so very awesome, and I know I'll be grateful for her guidance in the running of Brightlands.' She hesitated, then asked, 'Do you think she'll mind about us?'

'Mind? She'll be delighted. From the moment she set eyes on you she's bombarded me with dark hints that were little short of frank statements. Didn't I think it was time I settled down? Couldn't I see you're a lovely girl who'd be most suitable as the next mistress of Brightlands? Etcetera, etcetera. In fact, she'll consider this to be all her doing, and she'll be secretly proud of the way in which she's managed to bring it about.'

Robyn sighed happily. 'I hope I'll never disappoint her.'

They continued to lie close together on Alf's bed. Jonas's mouth, tender yet hungry, moved over hers until he paused to ask, 'You're still feeling okay? No dizziness at all, my dearest?'

'At first I was a little dizzy, but it's disappeared. Now I'm warm, contented, happy, excited, bewildered—even a little frightened at times. All those emotions are running through me in turn.' A shiver ran through her.

'You're frightened? Of Barbara, no doubt. I certainly underrated her.' Jonas moved his position so that he could gaze into her eyes. 'I'm making you a promise. Barbara will not set foot on this place again—ever.'

'That'll be difficult,' she pointed out. 'Your fathers are such old friends.'

'I don't care if they're blood brothers—I won't have her here. You haven't given me the exact details of what happened in the shed, but it's obvious she deliberately locked you in the coolstore.'

Robyn's eyes clouded. 'I don't want you to have trouble with the staff. I understand they like her, whereas I'm only a stranger.'

'They'll change their minds when they know I'm considering taking police action,' said Jonas, 'Barbara knew you wouldn't be able to open the door from the inside—in fact all the staff knew the state of the inside latch—and that makes her act a definite attempt on your life.' The tenseness of his voice indicated his fury.

'Let's forget her,' she said as she nestled against him. 'It's over now, although it was a black hour, that made me really scared. But isn't the darkest hour usually just before the dawn?'

His lips rested on hers for a long moment before he said, 'For us the dawn is rising, my beloved. It's the beginning of a new life. I shudder to think of your state if I hadn't come looking for you to give—good heavens, I almost forgot!' He sat up, put a hand in the pocket of his jacket and drew out a small box.

At first Robyn thought it was the box which had contained the signet ring Barbara had given him, but when he opened the lid she was almost dazzled by a bar of five diamonds. The sight of them made her gasp. 'An engagement ring? It's—it's *beautiful!*'

'I'm glad you like it.' He slipped it on to the third finger of her left hand, where it fitted perfectly. 'Holly helped me by telling me her size and advising me to get a size larger.'

Robyn gazed down at the ring. 'Holly knew about this?'

'Yes. I wanted to make the announcement during Christmas dinner. That's why I was so mad when Mother said she'd invited the Daltons. It would have been tactless to have announced it in front of them, because I know they've nursed hopes for Barbara and myself.'

She sent him a frank look. 'I couldn't help wondering about you and Barbara. Everyone seemed to think——'

'I've never loved Barbara, nor have I ever visited her room as she hinted,' he assured her. 'I'd have been an idiot to have done so. Surely you can work that one out for yourself?'

Robyn sighed happily, knowing that he spoke the truth. If he had been sufficiently unwise to go to her room Barbara would have had him in her grips at once.

Jonas said, 'My darling, there are still a couple of vital questions to be decided. The first is when shall we be married? Please don't keep me waiting too long.'

'As soon as it's possible,' she murmured, clinging to him in ecstasy, her cheek resting against his.

'Where? In New Zealand or in Australia?'

'New Zealand. Let's get married at Havelock North in that lovely church surrounded by all those large trees.'

'Right.' He stood up and pulled her to her feet. 'We'd better go and tell the others, or a search party will discover us in Alf's bed. But make no mention of Barbara's action. That'll come later.'

As Jonas had predicted, his parents were delighted. Flora embraced Robyn with genuine affection, telling her that at last they had a daughter.

Holly shed a few tears of happiness because she was so pleased with the way things had turned out. She hurried away to the room she was sleeping in that night and returned with her opal earrings, which she insisted upon Robyn accepting as an engagement present. 'In any case, I've left them to you in my will,' she said, 'so you might as well have them now. George would want you to have them,' she added.

Alf shook hands with Jonas. 'I've never seen you move so slowly, boss,' he declared frankly. 'For a while I was afraid you'd let the lassie get away back to Australia.'

Mrs Kerr said very little and Robyn realised that, with a new mistress at Brightlands, she was wondering about her job. She whispered to Jonas, who assured the housekeeper that Robyn would need her assistance and that the job was hers for as long as she wanted to keep it.

Flora then insisted that Robyn should ring her mother in Sydney. Rachel Burnett expressed her delight with the news and promised to fly to New Zealand for the wedding.

'Would you believe we're already unpacking the Easter bridal stock?' she exclaimed. 'The bridal gowns are all lovely, but there's one in particular that's really gorgeous. Fortunately it's your size. I'll bring it with me——'

Later, as Jonas held Robyn close to him on the upstairs balcony, the sun broke through the dark clouds. The pattern of bright rays streamed down to spread across the countryside like a golden fan. It's like an omen, Robyn thought. It's a glowing brightness on the years ahead.

Here's how to get this special offer from Harlequin!
As simple as 1...2...3!

AUGUST
TREASURY EDITION
COUPON

1. Each month, save one Treasury Edition coupon from your favorite Romance or Presents novel.
2. In four months you'll have saved four Treasury Edition coupons (<u>only one coupon per month allowed</u>).
3. Then all you have to do is fill out and return the order form provided, along with the four Treasury Edition coupons required and $1.00 for postage and handling.

Mail to: Harlequin Reader Service

RT1–A–2

In the U.S.A.
P.O. Box 52040
Phoenix, AZ 85072-2040

In Canada
P.O. Box 2800, Postal Station A
5170 Yonge Street
Willowdale, Ont. M2N 6J3

Please send me my FREE copy of the Janet Dailey Treasury Edition. I have enclosed the four Treasury Edition coupons required and $1.00 for postage and handling along with this order form.

(Please Print)

NAME_____

ADDRESS_____

CITY_____

STATE/PROV._____ ZIP/POSTAL CODE_____

SIGNATURE_____

This offer is limited to one order per household.

SUPPLIES LIMITED

This special Janet Dailey offer expires January 1986.

You're invited to accept
4 books and a
surprise gift _Free!_

Acceptance Card

Mail to: **Harlequin Reader Service®**

In the U.S.
2504 West Southern Ave.
Tempe, AZ 85282

In Canada
P.O. Box 2800, Postal Station A
5170 Yonge Street
Willowdale, Ontario M2N 6J3

YES! Please send me 4 free Harlequin Romance®novels and my free surprise gift. Then send me 6 brand new novels every month as they come off the presses. Bill me at the low price of $1.65 each ($1.75 in Canada)—an 11% saving off the retail price. There are no shipping, handling or other hidden costs. There is no minimum number of books I must purchase. I can always return a shipment and cancel at any time. Even if I never buy another book from Harlequin, the 4 free novels and the surprise gift are mine to keep forever.

116 BPR-BPGE

Name	(PLEASE PRINT)

Address	Apt. No.

City	State/Prov.	Zip/Postal Code

This offer is limited to one order per household and not valid to present subscribers. Price is subject to change.

ACR-SUB-1